ACCEPTANCE

CLUB X #5

K.M. SCOTT

Books by K.M. Scott

If I Dream (Corrupted Love #1)

Crash Into Me (Heart of Stone #1)
Fall Into Me (Heart of Stone #2)
Give In To Me (Heart of Stone #3)
Heart of Stone Volume One Box Set
Ever After (Heart of Stone #4)
A Heart of Stone Christmas (Heart of Stone #5)
Unforgettable (Heart of Stone #6)
Unbreakable (Heart of Stone #7)
Heart of Stone Volume Two Box Set

Temptation (Club X #1)
Surrender (Club X #2)
Possession (Club X #3)
Satisfaction (Club X #4)
Acceptance (Club X #5)
The Complete Club X Series Box Set

SILK Volume One
SILK Volume Two
SILK Volume Three
SILK Volume Four
The SILK Box Set

2017 Copper Key Media, LLC

Second edition

Published in the United States
ISBN-10: 1-941594-61-1
ISBN-13: 978-1-941594-61-2

Cover Design: Cover Me, Darling

Adult Content: Contains graphic sexual content

Life after Club X has been good for the three brothers who used to run Tampa's most exclusive fantasy club. Cassian and Kane run one of the city's up and coming restaurants, CK, and Stefan has his own successful bar in the old Club X building.

Two marriages, three kids, and three happy couples make up one big happy family.

But there's another son of Cassian March III out there, another illegitimate child who never knew his father. The three brothers don't agree that they should find him, and even more importantly, what they don't know about Sebastian could risk everything they cherish so dearly.

Chapter One

Kane

Cash rapped his knuckles on the bar and shook his head. "I don't like it, Kane. We've got a good thing going now. You've got two beautiful kids and a wife that adores you. I've got little Cassian and Olivia, and we've got a great thing here with this restaurant. The last thing we need is something that's going to change all that."

"I know. I'm not saying we should. I just think I know what—"

"Don't even think of it. You're an entirely different situation, and you know it."

I nodded, not entirely sure I agreed with him but not wanting to argue about this tonight. I'd hoped to get home early enough to find Abbi awake for the first time in over a week, and nothing was going to get in the way of spending at least a few minutes with the woman I loved.

Lifting my glass to my mouth, I swallowed the last of my drink and stood to leave. "Okay, Cash. We can table this for now, but the way Stefan was talking yesterday, I don't think it's going to sit for long."

Cash chuckled and slapped me on the back. "You leave Stefan to me. Go home and see your wife and kids and I'll see you Monday. Give everyone a kiss for me and Olivia, okay?"

"Same. I'll see you Monday bright and early."

As I headed toward the door, I heard Cash say, "Not too early. I do the Monday late nights. I'm thinking noonish. Maybe."

"Then maybe not bright and early," I joked.

I OPENED THE FRONT DOOR and quietly closed it so I didn't wake the baby. We'd finally gotten him to sleep through the night a few weeks ago, so my nightly routine mimicked something of a cat burglar. I tiptoed through the living room hoping to find Abbi, but I was too late. Exhausted like she was most nights, she probably gave up sometime around midnight.

I couldn't blame her. I just wanted to try to spend some time with her. We hadn't had a chance to be just the two of us in far too long. It would have to be another night, though.

Disappointed, I walked into the kitchen and opened the refrigerator only to stare into it for nearly a minute before closing the door. I wasn't really hungry. Not for food, anyway.

The kitchen light flickered on above me, and I

turned around to see Abbi standing in the doorway looking wide-awake and dressed in the t-shirt and boy shorts she always wore to bed.

"Did I wake him up again?"

She shook her head as she began walking toward me. "Nope."

Taking her in my arms, I pressed a kiss to her lips and let my hands roam down her back until I cupped her ass in my hands. "Everything okay?"

"I've been waiting for you," she said with a sexy smile. I hadn't seen that smile in far too long.

"Oh yeah? Did you find some magical way to get both Annalea and Liam to sleep at the same time?"

Her smile broadened, and she slipped my tie from around my neck. "Even better."

As her hands slowly unbuttoned my dress shirt, I wondered what could be better than having both kids asleep and some time to ourselves. Unsure what she meant, I waited until she'd finished with the buttons and slid my shirt off to ask.

"What's even better?"

Abbi moaned a tiny, sexy sound and ran her hands over my chest. "Alexandria took the kids for the night. We have until tomorrow afternoon to be just Kane and Abbi again, so what do you say we take advantage of it and head upstairs?"

I squeezed her ass in my hands and felt my cock grow hard. Over twelve hours to do whatever we wanted. I planned to take full advantage of every precious minute.

Nuzzling her neck, I inhaled the soft scent of honeysuckle on her skin. "I think a genie must have heard my wish because I was thinking we could spend a few minutes together tonight. It's been too long."

She scratched her fingernails down my bare back and moaned again. "It has, so let's get to that bed waiting for us."

By the time we made it to the bedroom, I'd stripped out of every stitch of clothing, but Abbi still wore those cute little underwear that made me wish every night when I got into bed that she wasn't as exhausted as I knew she was. Now that I had her all to myself, I planned on living out every fantasy I'd created since the last time we made love.

"I do love a man who's ready to go," she said with a smile as she inched back on the bed.

Looking down where her gaze sat, I had to agree. My cock and I were more than ready to go. Ready, willing, and able.

I leaned down and softly kissed the inside of her ankle. "This whole parenting thing puts a kink into my plans most nights, and not the good kind of kink."

"You know, I try to stay up every night, Kane. I do," Abbi said with a hint of sadness in her voice.

Looking up, I saw her mouth turned down in a frown. I kissed up her calf to her knee and nipped at the skin with my teeth, all the while keeping my gaze locked on hers. "I know. You don't have to say anything. It's just how it is. You're exhausted from being a mother. Believe me. I don't know how you do it."

Abbi smiled like it meant the world to her that I knew what she went through every day. In truth, I didn't. She was gone from our bed every morning when I woke up, getting Annalea ready for school and taking care of Liam's every need. By the time I left for work most days, she'd already put in hours to make sure our kids were fed, bathed, and ready for the day.

Being their father was a much easier job. I got to play with them before work and checked in on them to kiss them goodnight when I got home. That's not to say I never handled any of the dirty work with them, but nothing like what Abbi dealt with.

I flicked my tongue over the soft skin of her inner thigh and smiled up at her. "Tonight, you're not a mom or anything else but the woman I love."

"Mmmm, I like that."

My thumbs slid along the bottom of her pink and white polka dot boy shorts, teasing her with my touch as they inched closer to her pussy. She arched her back, signaling she wanted more than playful foreplay. Hooking my fingers, I tugged her panties off her body in one swift movement and felt my cock grow even stiffer.

I lowered my mouth to taste her as Abbi threaded her fingers through my hair, tugging hard with the first slow swipe of my tongue over her clit. Every cell in my body screamed for me to skip the slow shit and devour that delicious pussy. I wanted to taste every sweet inch of her. To bury myself in her and feel her come all over my face as my fingers fucked her until she begged me to stop.

The days of being that man who struggled to control every urge he felt were in the past, but it had been so long since Abbi and I had been together that remnants of that man now surged inside me.

Above me as I flicked my tongue inside her, Abbi whimpered and wriggled her hips. "Oh, God, that feels so good. I didn't realize how much I'd missed this."

Sliding two fingers into her, I lifted my head and smiled. "It's been way too long."

Her eyes fluttered closed at the feel of my fingers fucking her, and she nodded. "Oh, it has…"

I gently sucked her clit between my lips and pushed harder into her wet cunt until seconds later she came, drenching my mouth and fingers. As shudders wracked her body, I rode her release until she exhaled and the only movement left in her was the soft quivering of her thighs against my shoulders.

Sitting back on my heels, I looked down at the woman I loved and couldn't help think she was the most beautiful creature in the world. Flush with satisfaction from her orgasm, she lay there with her eyes closed looking like an angel. For a moment, I flashed back to the moment I met her and remembered how much I instinctively felt the need to protect her from that first second in Cash's office at Club X.

She'd always been my angel.

"You look a million miles away," she said softly, tearing me from my memories.

I shook my head to push them away. "Just thinking about how incredible you look."

"Oh, yeah? In my t-shirt lying here unable to move after what you just did?" she asked with a grin.

"Unable to move, huh? I think I'm going to have to see what I can do about that," I teased as I slid up her body.

Nudging my cock between her legs, I kissed her long and deep, my tongue sliding into her mouth like I wanted to slide into her cunt. Raking her fingernails down my back, she stopped me just as I moved my hips back, though.

Looking up into my eyes, she pushed against me. "Uh-uh. Turnabout's fair play."

"I like where this is going," I said with a grin. With the kids gone for the night, we were sampling the entire menu. I liked that.

She rolled me onto my back and kissed me. "Good. Now lay back and enjoy yourself."

Out of habit, I looked over toward the bedroom

door to see if the latch was closed. We'd tried this exact thing one night a few months ago and nearly got caught by Annalea. The next morning the latch went on the door.

As my mind traveled back to that night, Abbi kissed down over my stomach, pushing any ideas of anything other than her mouth on my cock right out of my head.

She stopped and hovered over me. Her fingers played with the studs I still kept in because she asked me to. With a devilish look in her eyes, she said, "I wonder how the ladies at school every morning would react if they knew your cock was pierced."

"Does that mean you want me to take them out?"

"No! I have very fond memories of these," she said as she stroked my cock from base to tip. "I wanted you from the moment you showed me them. I suspect that was the reason you got them in the first place, though."

I closed my eyes as she flicked her tongue over those studs, not wanting to tell her the real reason I got them all those years ago. Now wasn't the time to talk about how fucked up I'd been back then. I'd never told her the truth about them or many things about me from before I met her. I didn't want her knowing that man.

Abbi groaned against my skin as she slowly took my cock into her mouth inch by inch. I looked down and watched how her pink lips and tiny mouth swallowed all of me and then slowly pulled back to reveal my cock glistening from her. Her hand gripped the base and massaged as over and over she sucked me like it was something she couldn't get enough of. With every flick of her tongue and moment her soft lips slid over my skin, my angel inched me closer and closer to filling her.

I wanted to lift my hips and thrust hard into that beautiful mouth, fucking her like I would when I was between her legs. To ram my cock past her lips until it slammed against the back of her throat and those studs she loved so much made her gag. I knew if I did, though, I'd come in a second and I wanted this to last. I wanted this night to last.

So I remained still and watched as she took me to the edge and then eased me back, knowing exactly what to do with her tongue and her mouth each time. Finally, my body ached I wanted to come so badly, so I stuffed my hand into her hair, and tugging her head up gently, groaned, "No more teasing, angel."

Without a word, she lowered her head one more time and flicked her tongue along the vein that ran up the underside of my cock as she took all of me until those studs touched the back of her throat. Sucking hard, she bobbed up and down until I felt all control disappear and thrust my hips hard as I came, filling that pretty mouth that had given me what I'd dreamed of for weeks.

"I'm hoping that noise that came out of your throat when you came means you felt as good as I did when you went down on me."

I opened my eyes and smiled. "I know what you mean about not being able to move."

Abbi laughed at my joke and straddled my hips to sit on top of me. "So, does that mean we're done for the night? Because if that's the case, I'm okay with it. You are older than me."

Resting my hands on her hips to keep her from moving, I said, "Older than you? You make it sound like I'm some sugar daddy of yours. I'm not even eight years older, Abbi."

She leaned down to press a kiss onto my lips and whispered against them, "So you're saying you're up for more?"

As she spoke, she gently rubbed her pussy against my still hard cock, teasing me. I gripped her hips hard and nodded. "Be careful what you wish for, little girl. The big bad wolf might just surprise you with how much more he wants."

Abbi ran her tongue along her bottom lip and smiled. "Good. Let's see what you got for me, Mr. Wolf."

I flipped her over onto her stomach and covered her with my body before she knew what hit her. When she tried to get up onto her knees, I held her with my weight and whispered in her ear, "Still want more?"

Turning to look at me, she breathlessly said, "Yes."

Leaning back, I pulled her up by her hips so she sat on her hands and knees and encircled her neck with my hand. Rock hard and dying to be inside her, I closed my eyes and hesitated for a mere second before I let my need for everything she was take over.

I thrust forward, burying my cock inside her until she had every inch of me. A tiny moan escaped her throat, and then she gripped the sheets in her hands, her fingers grasping to hold on for what she knew was coming next.

With my hand still around her neck, I slammed into her body over and over like a wild animal. I needed to be inside her. I craved the feel of her clinging to me as I retreated, only to take all of me again a second later.

Abbi met my thrusts with her own, as wild and as needy as mine. It had been too long since we'd felt this way. Too many nights sleeping next to each other and not enjoying anything but rest. I didn't want that to be our lives, and neither did she. Tonight, we wanted to be the people we were when we first fell in love.

I sank my teeth into her shoulder and groaned, "Tell me what you want." It didn't matter that I knew the answer. I just loved to hear her say the words, and she knew it.

Grabbing my hair, she pulled hard and answered, "Fuck me. Fuck me like all I am is Abbi to you."

My brain heard fuck and set my body to the task. I pumped into her with everything I had and didn't slow down until I felt the first gentle squeeze of her cunt around my cock. She came in a rush, and I felt her strength leave her. One last thrust into her set off my release, and holding her to me, I came inside her.

Exhausted, we collapsed onto the bed, and when I could finally think again, I kissed the top of her head resting on my chest. "What did you mean to fuck you like all you are is Abbi to me?"

She stayed quiet for a minute before she said, "I didn't want to be your wife or Annalea and Liam's mother. I wanted to be that person you wanted that first night in your apartment on the top floor of Club X."

I turned her head so she could see my face. "You're always that to me, Abbi. Always. Do you think you're not?"

Her mouth turned down in a frown, and she shrugged. "I spend all day as the kids' mom, and when we're with your brothers and Olivia, I'm your wife. I just wanted to feel like that woman I was that night when you wanted nothing more than to be with me."

"You're always that to me," I said before I kissed her with all the love I felt for her.

Abbi traced tiny circles across my chest for a moment. "I also hoped it would make you remember who you were then too. I know you spend all day being that man Cash needs you to be. I know you want to be that man too, but I sometimes miss who you were when we met."

"That guy was so fucked up, Abbi. Why would you miss him over the man I am today?" I asked, wondering if we'd become what all married couples ended up being. I didn't want that for us.

She stroked my cheek and said, "I love everything you are, Kane. No man is a better father or husband. I just miss the guy who needed me like no one else ever had. I'm just afraid…"

"Afraid of what?" I asked as I looked down into her eyes to get a sense of what she meant.

Looking away, she mumbled, "Nothing. It's okay."

"Abbi, look at me. What are you afraid of? Whatever it is, I'm here and nothing will ever hurt you or the kids."

She turned her head back to face me and frowned. "I'm just afraid one of these days you're going to wake up and look at your life and hate it. When we first got together, we never talked about kids or you working like you do. You had a certain kind of life, and now it's all changed to a wife, two kids, a house, and a job that's nothing like what you used to do. I'm just afraid you'll decide you want something else. Someone else."

I stared at her in shock. Had we strayed that far from what we used to be in those early days that she doubted how much I loved her? Had we let the daily grind of married life do that to us?

Cradling her face in my hands, I shook my head. "I could never want anyone else. I never want you to doubt that. Ever. You are my life, Abbi. I would work my fingers to the bone if it meant you were happy. I love our kids. It never mattered to me that we didn't plan to have them. They're proof of how much we mean to each other."

Abbi sat up and forced a smile. "I'm sorry I said anything. You look upset. I didn't mean to do that."

I reached out and held her hand. "I'm not upset with you. If anything, I'm angry with myself for letting life get in the way of showing the most important person how much I adore her. I'm sorry, Abbi. I never meant to make you feel like I wasn't the happiest man on earth because I am. But now I'm wondering how you feel. Are you happy? The same thing about not planning to have two kids can be said about you too."

"No, don't think that! I love you, Kane. I love our children. I can't believe I said anything. Now you think I'm unhappy with my life and I'm not. I just wanted to feel like we used to again." She stopped for a moment and then said the words that stunned me. "I just didn't want you to forget that feeling we had in case you're thinking you could find it with someone else."

I felt like someone had hit me across the face. I didn't want anyone else. Christ, I couldn't imagine my life without Abbi. "Why would you think I'd want anyone but you?"

She hung her head and quietly said, "I don't know. Maybe I'm just stupid and jealous. Maybe it's because I'm here all day and you're at the restaurant looking like you do in your suit and tie. Maybe I'm just crazy. I don't know. I just worry that one day you're going to come home and say you don't want this anymore."

Taking her in my arms, I held her close and tried to fix whatever had made her think I didn't love her more than life itself. All this time I'd been disappointed we weren't having sex much anymore, but in her mind, it was so much more than that. She never came out and said it, but she thought I'd found someone else.

As she drifted off to sleep, her head resting on the spot over the heart that belonged to her, I hated this man I'd become. The business with Cash was a great success, but at what price?

CHAPTER TWO
CASSIAN

Y SON HAD HIS OWN idea about what sleeping in meant. Cassian and I shared a name, but we definitely didn't share the same opinion on what Sundays were for. While I would have liked to spend the morning in bed with his mother, two-year-old boys had a different agenda and by the time eight o'clock rolled around, he had begun banging his crib off the wall, his signal that the day needed to officially begin.

"He gave us a few extra minutes today," Olivia said with a smile as she sat up to answer our son's beckoning and pushed her long red hair off her face.

Scrubbing the sleep from my eyes, I looked over at the wall that separated our bedroom from his and tried to be thankful for those few minutes. For a few extra hours, I might have bought the kid a life-sized version of his favorite teddy bear, but for a few minutes I wasn't feeling that much thanks.

"Tell him I said next time if he can arrange for an hour I might buy him something," I grumbled as I buried my face in the pillow, knowing my time in bed had effectively ended for the day.

Olivia tapped me on the shoulder. "You know how I feel about spoiling him, Cash. No buying him things for more sleep."

As she walked out of the room, I said farewell to my sleeping in plans and threw the covers off to start my day. "We can call it his first job. He sleeps later, and I pay him. It's a win-win situation."

From the hallway, she yelled, "Nice plan, but no. Time to start the day, so I'll see you in the kitchen for coffee in a few, okay?"

Cassian banged his crib off the wall once more as Olivia opened his door, and I silently reminded myself I loved being a father. Just not at eight in the morning.

LESS THAN AN HOUR LATER, Olivia and I sat with Cassian in the living room playing with his favorite dinosaur toy. As he spent his time gobbling up the smaller dinosaurs around him, she said to me, "While you were in the shower, Abbi called."

I watched with amusement as the T-Rex exerted his dominance. "Yeah? You two doing something today?"

"I don't know. That's not why she called."

Something in Olivia's voice made me turn to face her, and I saw she had a look of worry in her eyes. "Is everything okay?"

Olivia sighed, knitting her brows. "She asked me

something very strange. I don't know what to think of it, though."

"Strange, huh? I'm intrigued. What's going on?"

Hesitating, she turned to look at our son and his dinosaur stomping on one with a pointy ridge down its back before sighing again and looking at me. "She asked me if I thought Kane was seeing someone else."

A laugh exploded out of me. Few questions were more ridiculous than that one. "Kane? No way. Nope."

Olivia narrowed her eyes in anger, a clear sign my response was not what she was looking for. "This is serious, Cash. She sounded upset."

"Honey, it's not serious. Kane is madly, completely, and blindly in love with Abbi. She could try to kill him and he'd forgive her. That's how much he adores her. The guy isn't seeing anyone else. Jesus, I don't even think he notices other women exist on the planet, Olivia. Trust me. She's barking up the wrong tree with this."

Concern for Abbi and Kane remained in her brown eyes, and Olivia frowned, unfazed by my explanation. "She says he's been getting calls and he lies to her about them. Cash, that's a sure sign there's another woman."

"Who's he say is calling?"

"Sometimes he says it's you or Stefan, and other times he claims it's the restaurant."

"The three of us call each other all the time. And it wouldn't be odd for the restaurant to call him. He is one of the owners and general managers."

Pushing her long red hair back with her fingers, Olivia nodded. "So you think it's all nothing even though he's lying about who's calling?"

I knew exactly what it was, but I didn't want to involve her in something I had no intention of bringing into our lives, so I forced a smile and hoped I could convince her it was just as I said. Nothing.

"I think my brother wouldn't even give another woman a look if someone held a gun to his head. It sounds like maybe Abbi's reading signs that aren't really there. Kane is as loyal as they come, strange phone calls or not."

For a moment, I wasn't sure Olivia believed me, but after I finished, she smiled and nodded. "I told her it was probably nothing to worry about, but I can't help but think something's wrong because he is lying, Cash. She knows that."

"How does she know? Did she check his phone?" I asked, suddenly wondering if Kane's sloppiness was going to make its way into my life with Olivia and Cassian.

A sheepish expression washed over my wife's face. "Don't tell him, please. She's just so worried. She's sure he's sleeping with another woman. I heard the fear in her voice, Cash."

As I promised not to tell my brother about his wife checking his phone, mentally I put it at the top of my list of things to do when I met with him and Stefan today. I'd indulged his curiosity or whatever it was for long enough.

"Well, tell her for me that he's not. I'm sure of it. The guy is like stone when it comes to everyone at the restaurant. I mean, he's nice enough, but I've seen women hit on him and it rolls off his back like water off a duck. He doesn't care. He's in love with Abbi, so he doesn't see other women. Maybe when I go over to Stefan's today you and Shay can take her out to lunch or something to take her mind off it."

A look of confusion settled into Olivia's face. "I didn't know you were going to your brother's today. I thought you and I were going to relax with the baby all day."

I turned to watch Cassian, who'd moved on from dinosaurs to his wooden puzzles of animals. "I have to go to Stefan's for a little while, but don't worry. It'll only be for an hour or so, enough time for you three to grab a nice lunch. I can even take the baby so you won't have to worry about the whole stroller thing."

Olivia got up from the couch and headed toward the kitchen. "No way. The last time he was with you and Stefan, he had a brand new word and the daycare administrator ended up pulling me aside to tell me he said booty about twenty times that day. I love Stefan, but he's a bad influence on my son."

I couldn't help but chuckle at the result of Stefan's

most recent experiment to get Cassian to say his name. Even after two years, the kid couldn't say it, even though he had no problem repeating anything else that came out of my brother's mouth. Two hours of trying to get him to say his uncle's name and all he'd gotten out of it was Stefan's use of the word booty once.

"Well, you can't say I didn't offer."

Behind me, she said, "And since you seem to have forgotten everything this morning, you know Shay and I can't take Abbi anywhere, especially if I'm trying to get her mind off the idea of Kane sleeping with another woman."

Sure I'd missed some part of the conversation when I was thinking back to my last boy's day out with Stefan and the baby, I shook my head in confusion and turned to look toward her standing at the kitchen island. "What are you talking about?"

Cassian suddenly seemed very curious about what his mother had to say too because he trotted over into the kitchen to join her. She gave him a bowl of dry cereal and sent him on his way with a kiss back to his toys. Grimacing, she waved me over to her, saying, "Little ears hear a lot, Cassian."

Clearly, I had missed something, so I headed into the kitchen. "What are you talking about? Why can't you and Shay take Abbi out to lunch?"

Whispering, Olivia explained, "Because Abbi has never gotten over the fact that when she was in the hospital giving birth to Annalea, Kane and Shay were getting drunk together in his apartment. She thinks they slept together."

Stunned, I opened my mouth to say something but couldn't. After a few seconds of processing the news that more than six years later, Abbi still hadn't forgiven Shay, I said, "I knew she was angry back then, but I had no idea she still harbored a grudge."

Olivia gave me a look like I was some kind of idiot for not knowing this information. "Cash, when can you say you've ever seen Abbi and Shay together at any time in the past six years? And haven't you ever noticed that as soon as Kane and Shay are anywhere close to one another at all at any get-together, Abbi's mood grows instantly dark? This couldn't have escaped your notice."

I thought back to the last few times we all got together at my mother's and had to admit Abbi and Shay never spoke even once. It hadn't been something that anyone had made a big deal of, though, so it hadn't seemed important.

"I guess, but they didn't sleep together. I know that for sure. Stefan wouldn't have been able to handle that."

Shaking her head, Olivia said, "It doesn't matter. She may have forgiven Kane, but she's never forgiven Shay. She knows they were close and she's jealous. So having Shay at lunch while I'm trying to convince Abbi that Kane would never want another woman isn't a good idea."

"Well, I guess I've been no help whatsoever with this, but thanks for bringing me up to speed on all the family dirt," I joked.

Olivia slid her arms around my waist and stood on her toes to kiss me. "You really are out of the loop, Cash. I still love you, though, even though you're perfectly clueless as to what goes on with your brothers."

I cradled her face and looked down into her dark eyes I so loved. "I've found being clueless when it comes to most of what goes on with my brothers is the best plan. You know, just in case the police get involved I can claim plausible deniability."

"Cute. So what time are you going to Stefan's?" she asked as Cassian ran up to us and hugged our legs.

"Mommy, can I have more cereal?"

As she filled his bowl, I said, "I'll head over there around ten. I don't see any reason why he should get to sleep in all day if I can't."

"Because he doesn't have any kids?"

I dismissed that idea with the wave of my hand. "No excuse. If we parents have to be up, Stefan can be up too."

"He'll love that. Let me know how it goes. I think I might take your suggestion about lunch with Abbi and the kids, so if I'm not here when you get back, I'll be with her."

Heading toward the shower, I thought about how wrong Abbi was. A tiny part of me wished that was what Kane was up to. Getting him to walk away from that would be easier.

AFTER TEN MINUTES OF BANGING on Stefan's door, I was treated to the sight of my younger brother in boxers staring out at me with a mixture of confusion and disgust. I knew I should have felt bad about waking him at that time of day on a Sunday, but I didn't.

"Wakey, wakey, baby brother. Kane will be here any moment," I announced as I pushed past him to get into his apartment.

"You've got to be fucking kidding me, Cash. What the fuck is with waking me up at the crack of dawn?"

One of his neighbors walked by and stared in shock at how he looked still holding the door open. Pointing toward the hallway to let him know, I joked, "I'm pretty sure your condo board is going to have a new issue on the agenda for the next meeting. She looked pretty freaked out seeing you that way."

He slammed the door shut and stormed past me to head back to his bedroom. "Fuck her. Like I give a damn what she thinks of how I look first thing in the morning. I don't even know her name. As for you, make yourself comfortable. I'll be up at noon."

"Kane's going to be here in a few minutes. Get yourself washed up and put some pants on, for fuck's sake."

Stefan turned to look at me and sneered. "You've got to be kidding me, Cash. Why can't this happen at a decent time of the day? I was at the club until nearly three this morning, and then Shay and I were up for hours when I got home. I'm dead ass beat, dude."

I thought about what Olivia had told me that morning about Shay and Abbi and asked, "Hey, have you guys spent a lot of time with Kane and Abbi? You know, dinner and things like that."

"What?"

"Did I stutter?"

Wide awake now, Stefan shook his head. "No, but that's not surprising since Abbi hates Shay for what happened between her and Kane. Why are you asking?"

I shrugged, understanding for the first time how truly clueless I was about family issues. "Olivia told me about that this morning. I had no idea."

"It's not a big deal. Shay understands why Abbi feels that way. She wishes things weren't like that, but she understands."

"And you're okay with it all?" I asked, curious how my equally as jealous brother felt about the whole situation.

"Okay with what? They didn't sleep together, so there's nothing to be okay with. Now if you don't mind, you've wasted enough of my day with nonsense. I need a shower if I'm going to have to deal with you and Kane, so make yourself comfortable and make me some goddamned coffee, okay?"

Left alone with my orders, I started his coffee maker and took a seat on his couch. Kane knocked a few minutes later and joined me to wait for Stefan. He looked like he'd had a rough night. Hell, he didn't even look like he'd shaved that morning. Kane shaved every day, so something was up.

"Man, you look like hell. I thought you were going to try to spend some time with Abbi last night. Did you two decide to go on a bender?" I asked as I studied the dark circles under his eyes.

"Rough night sleeping."

Typical Kane answer. Short and to the point. Curious to know if he knew about his wife's feelings about Shay, I said, "Olivia told me she might get together with Abbi and Shay for lunch today."

His eyebrows shot up in surprise. "Really? All three of them?"

Rolling my eyes, I said, "Jesus, am I the only person who didn't know about the thing between Abbi and Shay?"

My frustration at being out of the loop with family gossip seemed lost on Kane, who shrugged and leaned back against the couch. "I guess."

His indifference to my newfound information irritated me for some reason I wasn't sure I understood, so I decided to drop a little bombshell of my own on him. "You know, she's pretty sure you're cheating on her."

Kane sat up straight, his eyes wide, and he shook his head. "What the fuck are you talking about?"

"She thinks you're stepping out on her. She told Olivia. I guess she knows you've been lying to her about the phone calls you've been getting. Pretty sloppy, if you ask me, Kane."

He winced and took a deep breath, blowing the air out slowly. "Well, that explains a lot."

"I told you this whole thing was going to be trouble."

"I didn't think it would start affecting my marriage, for God's sake."

I smacked him on the shoulder as I stood up to get myself a cup of coffee. "The road to hell is paved with good intentions, Kane. You should know that better than anyone else, I'd think."

Stefan appeared once again, this time dressed in jeans and a t-shirt, and made a beeline for his morning coffee. "Hey, Kane. Thanks for agreeing to ruin my fucking Sunday. You want to remind me again why I should care one fuck about this whole thing?"

"Nice to see you too, Stef. Are we alone?"

Looking around in confusion, Stefan poured milk into his mug and nodded. "Like it would matter? I don't see Shay dialing up Abbi to share whatever we say. Anyway, she's gone already, so yes, we're alone to have our little boys club meeting."

"Are you going to be this cranky the whole time?" I asked as I sat down next to Kane, amused at how irritable waking up a few hours early made our younger brother.

He took a gulp of coffee and pointed at the two of us. "Go to hell, Cash, yes I am, and screw you and your whole thing about family being so important that we have to deal with this at all, Kane."

I looked at Kane and laughed. "I love it when we get together for these talks with him. Interventions go better than this."

Kane smiled and nodded as Stefan joined us in his living room. He took another drink of coffee and raised the mug in the air. "At least with an intervention it would involve me enjoying myself. Nothing about this whole brother thing has been fun in the least. So if we could get this moving since you got my ass out of bed early, I'd really appreciate it."

The time had come to do something about our problem.

Chapter Three

Stefan

MY BROTHERS LOOKED OVER AT me like I had some answer to solve our problem. Who the hell was I? The March Family therapist? As if I knew what to do.

"Don't expect me to start this. I'm still on the fence about if I even want to be involved."

Cash's face brightened at my words and he nodded his head. "See, that's what I'm saying. This isn't something we need to get wrapped up in, Kane. Best to leave sleeping dogs lie."

"This isn't a dog, Cash. This is family."

As usual, Kane had a way of saying very little but enough to make the situation seem far more serious than I preferred. Cash didn't seem to appreciate Kane's succinct summary of the issue either.

"Maybe, Kane. Right now, all we have is some guy claiming to be the son of our father," Cash said, practically dismissing the idea of this stranger being anything close to family.

"You mean like I was way back when?" Kane said sharply. "I was in the same place this guy is, so I know how he feels. He's just reaching out to us probably because he wants to get to know his brothers."

Rolling his eyes, Cash sat back on the couch. Kane did seem particularly sensitive about this topic, I had to admit. I guess I could understand. Sort of. I'd always known who I was, just like Cash. We were Cassian March's sons. For the first two decades of my life, we were the only sons. Then Kane came into our lives and to get our father's money, we had to work together. It had been rocky for a while at first, but eventually we saw him like we did each other.

As a brother, pure and simple. No half attached. Just our brother.

The problem is we were younger when he came around. And if we were being truthful, we had a good reason to accept Kane. Now there was nothing making us take a chance on yet another child of our father's.

"I wonder if it's that innocent, Kane," I said, still not sure how I felt about this brand new family member who wanted to get to know us.

He looked at me and then Cash and frowned. "What are you two afraid of? Maybe he just wants to get to know the people he's related to."

Cash screwed his expression into a grimace. "And maybe he thinks he's found the pot of gold at the end of the rainbow and plans to cash in on having our father's DNA. That's assuming he's even our real brother. I just don't see any upside to this for us."

"His name is Sebastian. Maybe we should start calling him by name if he's going to be family," Kane continued, clearly undeterred by Cash's reluctance to even meet with the guy.

"Fine. Let's just go get him, put him in the spare bedroom at my place, and we can all be one big happy family," Cash snapped.

Assuming a rare role between my two older brothers, I tried to diffuse the situation before Kane launched at him and tried to convince him that way. "Whoa, let's keep calm, okay? Cash, I'm sure Kane doesn't want Sebastian to move in with you or even be that big a part of our lives right from the get-go. And Kane, I think you can understand why Cash is hesitant to open this can of worms with someone we don't even know. Maybe we should just calm the hell down, okay? Deep breaths, guys."

Both of them leaned back on the couch, their arms folded across their chests and frowns on their faces. I had a sense that while they weren't barking at each other, they weren't exactly seeing eye-to-eye yet on this newfound brother of ours just yet, even after hearing my wonderful brotherly advice.

Cash took a deep breath and slowly let his arms fall away to his sides. "Fine. What do we know about him? Maybe we should talk about that first. If I knew something about him, I might not be so dead set against meeting him."

"What do we know about Sebastian?" Kane asked, subtly jabbing Cash with the fact that he still hadn't even called the guy by name yet.

"Fine. What do we know about Sebastian?"

Looking over toward me, Kane sat up and eased his own body language. "Okay, we know his name is Sebastian Thorne and his mother is someone named Sandra Thorne. Other than that, I don't know much yet. My guy is still checking him out. So far, he hasn't found anything that says he's a gold digger, if that's what you're worried about, Cash."

"What I'm worried about is upending my life, my very happy life with Olivia and my son, because our father may have fathered this person."

Cash certainly didn't have any problem explaining what bothered him.

"What else did you find out, Kane?" I asked, suddenly curious about this Sebastian guy. "What's he like? Where's he live? How old is he?"

My interest surprised him, and for a moment he looked a little shocked to hear me say anything, probably because I hadn't taken a side one way or another since this whole new brother thing began almost two weeks ago. Unlike my older brothers, I preferred to take time to think things over.

"Well, this is all I know so far. He looks like Cash

and me. Black hair and blue eyes. I guess he got our father's genes in that. My guy says he's twenty-six and works as a bartender at a place in Dade City. He lives with a girl, but from what my guy has seen, he's not exactly the loyal type."

I chuckled at Kane's description of the guy. "He sure as hell sounds like one of us. Well, not you, Kane, but Cash, you have to admit he sounds like us."

Cash gave me a sneer. "Being a manwhore doesn't mean he's our brother, Stef."

"I didn't say it did. I just think maybe we should find out more before we put the kybosh on this whole thing. This Sebastian guy might be okay."

"And he might be a money-grubbing gold digger who thinks he's found three ATM machines ready and willing to cough up money," Cash answered.

Kane's frustration boiled over, and he nearly launched from his seat on the couch. Storming toward my balcony, he mumbled something about needing some air and left. Nothing had caused a rift between the three of us like this threatened to since our early days at the club, and I wondered if this thing with some supposed long-lost brother was going to tear our family apart.

For his part, Cash didn't seem to be swayed by Kane's rare show of emotion about the subject. Shaking his head, he sighed and said, "You know, I get why he feels this way. I do. He sees a lot of himself in this guy, and maybe that's right. You and I have always known from the time we were born that we were dad's kids. There was never any question, and nobody had to give us the title of Cassian March's sons. I just worry what this Sebastian could do to the lives we have now."

"What could he really do, though?" I asked, unsure what some stranger could change about our lives. "It's not like acknowledging he's our brother is going to mean we have to do anything for him."

Worry etched into Cash's face. "I don't know, but I worry. The last time we found out about a brother, we had to work with him, even though we didn't want to then. That it turned out good doesn't change the fact that our lives were turned upside down for a while. I'm not sure I want that to happen again."

"Cash, that was different. Dad's will forced the three of us to accept each other. It was his way of making things right, and even though it was hard in the beginning, look at us now. I think it could be okay to find out if this Sebastian is really our brother, and this is coming from the youngest who would have to give up his cherished spot as the baby of the family."

My attempt at lightening the mood failed, and Cash asked a question I hadn't thought of before. "Why didn't Dad ever mention another son in anything on his death? The will doesn't say a thing about him. He obviously wanted us to know about Kane, so why not another son?"

I heard the glass door to the balcony close behind me, and before I could answer Cash, Kane spoke up. "I don't see what our father mentioning in his will has to do with anything. It doesn't mean Sebastian isn't our brother."

Afraid of another clash between them, I answered Kane before Cash had a chance to speak up. "It might mean he isn't our brother at all. It does seem like a pretty big oversight to not remember a fourth son when you remember a third, don't you think?"

He didn't answer. Instead, he sat down on the couch and crossed his arms again. That breath of fresh air hadn't changed much, it seemed.

When he finally did begin to speak again, he wasn't as eager to fight as a few minutes before but still wouldn't let go of the idea of finding out all we could about our new potential brother. Running his hand over the top of his head, he spoke slowly, like he was choosing his words carefully.

"I admit it seems odd that our father chose to acknowledge me and not another son he may have had. I'll give you that. But I don't see the harm in just finding out about the guy. If he isn't our brother, then we've lost nothing. If he is, though, I don't see why he shouldn't have the chance to at least know he's got family in us."

Neither Cash nor I said anything in response for a long moment. Looking over at him, I knew he had something to say, though, even if he was trying not jump all over Kane's suggestion.

Taking a breath, Cash nodded and smiled. "All I'm worried about is the potential damage he could do to our lives. That's all I've been saying. I just don't trust the fact that some guy out of the blue begins contacting you wanting to know if we're his brothers. I don't need some relative looking for a handout instead of truly wanting to know us. Or even worse, I don't want some stranger bringing shit into our lives. Family's a dicey thing, Kane. Adding someone new to the dynamic, someone who comes with their own baggage, isn't something I'm looking to do right now."

We seemed to be at an impasse, but I couldn't say I completely agreed with Cash. I wasn't sure I wanted some strange guy's shit being dumped into my lap either, but I was curious enough to want to know more before I walked away from this Sebastian person.

Pursing his lips, Kane looked like he wanted to start arguing again, so before he did that and those two came to blows, I said, "Cash, I feel your problem with this, but I'm with Kane. I say we feel this thing out a little more. If it turns out bad, at least we found out the truth."

My support surprised Kane, but I saw by the look in Cash's eyes he was disappointed with my decision. He stood to leave and said, "Okay, but I'm going to stay out of it until I hear something that makes me believe he's really our brother. If you can give me proof, and I mean real proof that he's one of us, I'll decide then how much I want of him in my life. Until then, I want no part of this."

He left without another word. Kane sat staring at me, still shocked I'd sided with him. What could I say? Curiosity got the best of me.

"I didn't think you'd want to find out if Sebastian is our brother, Stef. To be honest, I thought you'd be the one I had to convince since you hated finding out about me in the beginning."

Kane wasn't wrong. I resented him so fucking much when he came into our lives. Suddenly, I'd gone from being one of two sons of Cassian March to one of three, and even more, I was the one who seemed to matter the least. Then when our father decreed that for us to receive any of our inheritance we had to all work together to be successful at some business, I hated Kane. If it wasn't for him, Cash and I would've just gotten what we'd been promised and lived happily ever after.

But that's not how it went, and all these years later, I couldn't say I was unhappy about that anymore. Sure, there was a lot of ugliness along the way, but we came out of it all as brothers, like my father had hoped.

"Yeah, well, I've grown up a lot since you came on the scene. I'm not saying I want another brother, but I'm not saying I don't. All I'm saying is let's see what he's all about."

"Why is Cash so against this, though?"

I wasn't sure of the exact answer, but I had a guess. "Cash is a businessman, first and foremost. He thinks in money terms more than we do. He only sees the potential liability some new heir of our father's could present us. Security means a lot to Cash."

"I don't want this to affect Abbi and the kids in any way either, so I'm not that different from him. I just can't understand not even finding out."

Standing, I patted Kane on the shoulder as I passed on my way to the kitchen to get more coffee. "You see yourself in this. This guy is where you were all those years ago."

He thought about what I said before heading toward the door to leave. "So what do you see in this?"

"I'm not sure, but my curiosity is piqued so I'm on board with it. If it turns out like Cash is worried it will, I'll walk away from this whole thing and not look back. My issue isn't security. Mine is dealing with bullshit and drama, neither of which I need in my life. If that's what this Sebastian comes with, he best stay away because I'm past that."

A slow smile spread across Kane's face. "Where did that punk ass guy I more often than not wanted to pound the shit out of go, Stef?"

"He grew up, jackass. Tell Abbi we said hi and bring those kids with you next time. I like them."

Kane smiled in that way I knew was genuine. "Tell Shay I'm sorry I didn't get to see her this time."

As the door closed, I couldn't help but notice the difference between what I said about Abbi and what he said about Shay. Cash was right about family. It was a dicey thing.

✕

"STEFAN, YOU HOME?" SHAY CALLED out as she came into the apartment.

I looked up from the couch where I was lounging out like I should on a Sunday afternoon and held out my hand to grab her as she passed. "Right here, baby. You're back early."

She smiled and came over the back of the couch to lie on top of me. After a sexy kiss that made me want to forget about any more talking, she said, "I was actually done much earlier, but I didn't want to interrupt the March brother pow-wow."

Sliding my hands down her back to cup her perfect ass, I pulled her against my quickly hardening cock and groaned. "I don't know why. Cash and Kane would have been fine with you here while we talked."

"Well, I figured I'd let you guys have your man time," she teased while she pushed her hips forward, pressing the front of her jeans into my cock.

"I prefer this kind of man time. What do you have planned for today?" I asked as I slid my hand up under her t-shirt to unhook her bra.

"Not sure. Why?"

"Because I'm in the mood for some easy like Sunday afternoon fucking."

Shay gave me a wink and sat up on my legs to wriggle out of her t-shirt and bra. Throwing them onto the nearby chair, she cupped those gorgeous breasts of hers in her hands and smiled down at me.

"Hmmm, I think I might be able to fit you into my schedule. I have two others this afternoon, but I'll make room for you."

I pulled her down on top of me and kissed her hard. "Two others? I don't share well with others, baby."

She rubbed against my hard cock and giggled. "I guess I'm going to have to tell them I can't service them then because my boyfriend is being difficult."

Hooking my thumbs in the waist of her jeans, I pulled them down her legs and she kicked them off onto the floor. I made quick work of her silk panties, nearly tearing them off her body, so she was naked against me.

"You can tell them I'm very difficult. It's one of the reasons you love me."

As my finger slid through her wet slit, she moaned, "Uh huh. Very difficult."

Her mouth pressed hard against mine as I continued to finger her, and she flicked the tip of her tongue against my tongue in that way that never failed to make me go crazy. Quickly pushing my jeans and boxers down so my cock was free, I grabbed her hips and held her tight as I slid into her hard and fast.

My desire to fuck her took over, and I pumped into her as she rolled her hips against me and kissed me like my mouth held the only thing she ever wanted. Even after all our years together, Shay and I were still the same two people who couldn't get enough of one another, even on a lazy Sunday afternoon.

She rode me like my cock was hers to use, and I loved it. I loved her, probably more than she knew. Sure, we said I love you all the time, but over the years I'd come to realize that meant more than romance and sex.

Shay was the only woman I could imagine being with for the rest of my life. We never talked about it or mentioned marriage, but I knew it. A piece of paper wouldn't change how I felt about her. She was the woman for me.

With one last thrust into her tight cunt, she came apart, milking my cock to my own release, and then in the middle of the afternoon we lay there in each other's arms not caring about anything but each other. It wasn't what my brothers had, and I didn't care. They had their happiness, and I was happy for them.

But Shay and I had ours too.

As I lay there lost in thought about how good she

felt next to me, she asked, "So how did the meeting go? Are you guys going to see what's up with this guy who claims he's one of your father's kids?"

I shook my head to get rid of my thoughts about us and nodded. "Yeah. Well, Kane and I are. Cash isn't interested so far."

Shay kissed me softly on the lips and smiled. "I think it's a good idea. Who knows? He might be someone you can hang out with. Someone like you who isn't married like Cash and Kane."

Chuckling at the idea, I kissed her on the forehead. "I can't believe I'm saying this, but I think I'm too old to be hanging out anymore with twenty-six year olds. Those days are long gone."

Her eyebrows shot up in surprise. "I can't believe it. The legendary Stefan March has officially become an adult. You better watch out. Who knows what that will bring?"

She was right. If I didn't watch myself, one day I'd be thinking I should be like Cash and Kane.

Chapter Four

Kane

AFTER GETTING THE GREEN LIGHT, at least from Stefan, I headed over to John Kearney's to see what else he'd found out about Sebastian. The guy worked seven days a week since his wife left him for some insurance salesman from Orlando and practically lived at his hole-in-the-wall office if he wasn't out in the field investigating, so I had a pretty good shot at finding him sitting behind that old wooden desk of his.

John looked up when he heard the office door open and waved me in. "Kane, what brings you here on a beautiful Sunday afternoon? I don't think I've found out much more since I last talked to you."

I sat down in front of his desk and looked at him, trying to figure out if he'd even bothered going home the night before. His face hadn't been touched by a blade in what looked like days, and his brown hair looked like it needed a good washing by the way it hung down in his eyes. Hell, it needed a good trim too.

"Living here now, John?" I asked half-jokingly.

He looked around at the drab tan walls surrounding us and laughed. "No, why?"

"You look like shit, man. When was the last time you left here?"

Running his hand over his chin, he shrugged. "Life of a single guy."

How different he looked since I met him all those years ago when I first needed someone to check out people at Club X. Back then, he was a married man with a young wife and looked like he was on top of the world. Now all I saw was the empty shell of that guy. He sounded the same, but there was something missing in him these days.

"I guess the life of a single guy doesn't involve a shower or a razor."

"Beards make women go wild these days. Haven't you seen all those young douchebags with them? The chicks dig it. It's like carte blanche to look like a goddamn scumbag. It's a good time to be a lazy guy. You should try it."

I shook my head and cringed at the idea of any woman digging John like this. "Yeah, no. Not my thing."

"Your loss. You're married anyway, so what do you care about what attracts the ladies, right?"

"I don't. What I care about is finding out what more you know about this person who claims he's a son of Cassian March."

John nodded and blew the air out of his lungs slowly. "Well, I still haven't found any legal proof he's your brother. His birth certificate only lists the mother's name. And I've found no real evidence that your father ever recognized him as a child of his. I can say this, though. I've seen him and damnit if he doesn't look like you and Cassian. Those must have been some serious genes your father was toting around with him. I wonder what happened with Stefan, though."

I thought about Alexandria and how strong she was and chuckled. "You've never met his mother. Something tells me her genes are just as serious."

Whatever I said must have struck him as funny because he burst out laughing like we'd been telling jokes for the past five minutes. "Interesting family you guys have."

"So did you find out anything else about this guy?"

John shook his head. "Other than his name, where he lives, and where he works, all I know so far is he doesn't seem to have any legal claim to being Cassian March's son. It has only been two days since I started this case, though, so I expect I'll find out more this week."

"Okay. Let me know as soon as you find anything out."

I stood to leave as he promised to call me the minute he got any new information on Sebastian Thorne. Thanking him, I turned to leave and stopped.

My curiosity wanted more satisfaction. Looking back at John, I said, "How about giving me the addresses of his place and his work?"

A sly grin slowly spread across his face. "Want to check him out for yourself, huh?"

"Yeah. Can't hurt to look."

As he scribbled down the addresses on a sheet of paper, he nodded. "Nope. Just a warning, though. He's like the mirror image of you. There's no way he's not going to recognize you if he sees you, so lay low."

"You think he hasn't seen me or my brothers yet? He contacted me, not the other way around."

John handed me the paper. "That's true. I guess he probably has taken a gander at you already. Still, I think it would be better if you lay low on Frisco with this guy. Look, but don't touch."

"Got it. I'll keep that all in mind. Thanks, John. Let me know when you find out anything else."

"Of course. You'll be hearing from me soon, hopefully."

✕

"MOMMY! LIAM POOPED AGAIN AND it's awful!"

Annalea's announcement that her brother's diaper was dirty greeted me as I walked back into the house. From the kitchen, Abbi yelled out, "I'll be right there, honey."

I picked up my son from the playpen as Annalea

showed me a picture she'd drawn. "Daddy, look what I made at Grandma's. Guess what it is."

My eyes teared up as the smell wafting up from Liam's diaper nearly overwhelmed me, so all I saw was a blurry flower or maybe a rainbow. Taking my best guess, I answered, "That's a beautiful flower picture, honey. I'll take a better look as soon as I get your brother changed."

Abbi met me as I began to climb the stairs. "Kane, I didn't realize you were home. Everything okay at the restaurant? Did you find out what the problem was with the electricity?"

Remembering the lie I'd told her about where I was going hours earlier, I forced a smile and nodded. "Everything's okay. Just a problem with one of the breakers. I'll be right back down. Just need to clean up a mess with this little guy."

Thankfully, I got away before she could ask me any more questions about the nonexistent problem at CK. As I changed Liam's diaper, I stared down into his dark blue eyes so similar to mine and told myself my lies weren't really anything that could hurt anyone. I just wanted to keep the whole business with this potential new brother away from my family until I knew one way or another what kind of person he was.

That wasn't a bad thing, was it?

Liam smiled up at me, likely thankful that I'd helped him out of wearing shit, and I lifted him off the changing table to give him a kiss. "Feel better, little man? What do you say we go back downstairs and see the ladies in our life?"

Before we could get out of the room, though, Abbi appeared in the doorway with a look on her face that told me she wanted to talk. All I could hope was she didn't ask more questions that would force me to lie again.

"Do you want me to take him?" she asked sweetly, her arms out to take hold of Liam.

But I didn't want to give him up just yet. I didn't get too many chances to hang out with my son, and I liked to take advantage of the time I got.

"No, I have him. Is it time for him to eat?"

"In a little bit." She took his hand and pretended to nibble on his fingertips. "Who gets pears today? Yum, yum, yum, yum, yum. Does my little man love his pears?"

Liam smiled at her playing with his hand, and Abbi smiled back at him like he was the light of her life. I loved watching her with the kids like this. That's why I wanted to protect this part of my life from anything that could hurt the ones I loved.

Abbi looked up at me and said, "He looks more like you every day. Compared to when Annalea was a baby, he's like the polar opposite."

"It's the black hair. He got the March genes. She got yours," I said as I guided her toward the hallway.

"Annalea's alone, isn't she? We should go downstairs."

She touched my arm to stop me, and I turned around to see that look again. "She's okay, Kane. Is something wrong? You're acting weird."

"Nothing's wrong. I'm fine." I bent down to kiss her softly on the lips. "I had a great time last night, by the way."

"I did too," she said as her cheeks blushed a gentle pink. "I don't know if we should be talking about this in front of the baby."

I looked at Liam, who sat in my arms blissfully unaware that his parents were talking about the great sex they had the night before. "I think we're safe, angel. Our little man here understands nothing yet."

Abbi touched my arm again, and I turned to see her staring up at me like I'd just said the most wonderful thing she'd ever heard. "It's been a long time since you called me that."

I knew exactly what she meant. Between work, a new baby, and getting used to having two kids, it had been a very long time since I'd been much of anything but someone's boss or someone's father. I wanted to change that, though.

"I know, and I'm sorry. I've been too busy at work and with everything happening after Liam was born, but I'm going to make sure I'm more than just the guy who sleeps here from now on. I promise, Abbi."

She looked at me with wide eyes full of concern.

"Okay. Is there something I should know, Kane? You're sort of making me wonder what's going on with you."

I really didn't want to have this conversation. "I'm fine. There's nothing wrong, Abbi."

Liam thankfully got antsy in my arms and cried out, breaking the tension and giving me an excuse to walk away, even though I knew Abbi had more to say. The problem was she wasn't going to just let this go.

As much as I wanted to be wrong, by the time I reached the kitchen and put Liam into his high chair, Abbi was right beside me with that same questioning look in her eyes. As I turned to get the baby's lunch, she said, "I think maybe we should talk, Kane. Okay?"

Pretending to be busy picking just the right glass jar of pureed green vegetables, I said nothing as I grabbed peas and pears and the feeding spoon. I pulled a chair from the table and sat down in front of Liam, who was completely oblivious to the tension growing between his mother and father at that moment.

"Ready for some delicious peas, little man?" I asked with as much enthusiasm as I could muster for the gooey green goop I'd scooped out of the jar.

"Kane, are you ignoring me or didn't you hear me when I said I wanted to talk?"

Liam gobbled up the spoonful of peas and then proceeded to dribble half of it down his chin and onto the blue and green bib with caterpillars Abbi had put on him. Thoroughly pleased with himself, he banged his hands on the highchair tray and kicked his legs out as he squealed for more food.

"You must really love this," I said as I directed another spoonful of peas at his mouth.

He repeated his drooling act, this time keeping even less in his face than before. I wiped his mouth, feeling Abbi's stare practically boring a hole through the side of my head.

"I'm not ignoring you. I just figured it was time for Liam to eat. If you want to talk, that's fine. We can talk, Abbi."

My words might have seemed a bit more truthful if I'd bothered to look at her when I said them, but I was pretty sure she'd see right through my lies if she got a look at my eyes.

"Fine, then let's talk. Maybe you can even face me too."

There was no missing her meaning there. I took a deep breath and turned to look at her, but I didn't see the angry glare I thought I would. Instead, I saw a look of pure fear in her eyes, the kind someone got when they were afraid they were about to lose everything that meant the world to them.

Christ, I didn't want it to be like this. I wasn't lying just to get my jollies. I never lied to Abbi, except about things that could hurt her. But I hated seeing how frightened she was by how I was acting.

"Kane, I don't know what's going on, but my gut says something is. What's wrong? Are you unhappy with me? With our life? It seems like every time I look into your eyes I see something that says you don't want to be here anymore."

Hearing those words made me feel like someone was punching me in the heart. I put the spoon in the jar of baby food and took her hands in mine, wishing whatever I said next would erase the fear and sadness in her face.

"I love you, Abbi. You and the kids are my life. I wouldn't trade this for anything. I hate that you even thought I wasn't unbelievably happy with what we have here."

"Then why do you seem so preoccupied in the past few weeks? I was so sure you found someone else that I asked Olivia about it. She thinks I'm crazy. Maybe I am, but I've never seen you like this before. So I'm asking you now. Is there someone else?"

My chest hurt at the thought of any other woman other than Abbi for me. "No. I don't want anyone else. Not from the moment I fell in love with you, which was about ten seconds after meeting you. You know that."

Liam squealed for more peas, so Abbi fed him another spoonful and then crouched down in front of me. Looking up into my eyes, she said, "Even now as you're telling me there's no one else, you have that look in your eyes. I've never seen you look like this, Kane. It's like a look of need, and it scares the hell out of me because I'm worried one of these days you're going to come home and tell me you're leaving."

I wanted to tell her I knew what that look was from. I'd seen that very look in my eyes every time I looked in a mirror growing up. It came from knowing a part of my life was absent. Then it was because of my father, and now it was the possibility that I had another brother out there, another person like me who had been ignored all his life and never seen for who he truly was.

But until I knew he wasn't like the person I'd been back then, I wouldn't risk bringing him into my life in any way that involved Abbi and the kids.

Cradling her face, I tried to ease her mind and show her the look in my eyes was nothing. "I'm crazy in love with you, and every day I love you more, angel. I don't want anyone else. There's only you for me. You're my life. Without you and the kids, I'd have no reason to live. It's that simple. Whatever you're seeing in my eyes, believe me, it has nothing to do with how much I love you and our kids. I'm sorry you thought I was unhappy. I'm not."

She let out a heavy sigh as tears filled her eyes. "I was so worried you'd gotten tired of this life and wanted something else, Kane. I told you that last night, and I meant it. I just want you to know if this isn't what you want to do with your life, if you don't want to run the restaurant or live in this house anymore, I'll be right by your side with what you want to do. I'm not afraid of change as long as we're together. Just keep that in mind."

I leaned forward and kissed her gently, loving the feel of her lips on mine. "My work and where we live are things I can live without. You and the kids I can't, though. You're the most important parts of my life. You're my family."

"We'll always be there for you, Kane. I love you and the kids love their father. Never forget that."

Liam let out another cry to let us know he wanted more of his lunch, and while Abbi finished feeding him, I watched the woman I adored tend to him and hoped someday soon I'd be able to tell her what that look in my eyes was about.

I may not have realized it until my own father died, but family was more important than anything else in the world.

Chapter Five

Stefan

THE PARKING LOT OUTSIDE THE CocoNut Restaurant and Bar began to empty out as the minutes ticked toward midnight. Kane and I had sat there in his Mustang for nearly two hours trying to get a look at Sebastian Thorne. The PI my brother paid to do just this kind of thing had told him he'd be off work at ten, yet there we sat in his incredibly uncomfortable car staring at the doors of the building hoping to see him.

"Tell me again why John couldn't just take a friggin picture of the guy and we could see what he looks like that way? I swear you and that guy are stuck in the seventies," I mumbled as I watched out the passenger side window for any sign of the person who might be our brother.

"You didn't have to come, Stefan. I never asked you to, in fact. All I said was I was coming here tonight. You invited yourself."

I turned to look at Kane and gave him a well-deserved sneer. "Whatever. That doesn't answer the question of why John couldn't do this. It is his job, you know. This is just the kind of thing he's supposed to do. Instead, he's comfy at his house while my ass feels like it's about to fall asleep from sitting in this damn relic of yours. Why didn't you use the SUV you guys own?"

"Because it has the seats for the kids and if Abbi needs to take them anywhere she needs that car." Reaching for the radio, he turned up a Led Zeppelin song and said, "Now if you're done questioning me on things that have nothing to do with what we're doing here."

I threw him another sneer and turned my head back toward the window to continue the Sebastian watch. I knew why Kane had taken the Mustang instead of the SUV. He still hadn't told Abbi one damn thing about this whole potential brand new brother business. Well, that and he loved this car like it was one of his kids. Why I had no idea. He made more than enough money to afford a brand new car instead of something that was over forty years old. To hear him talk, it was better than anything Cash or I owned, but at the moment, my sore ass made me disagree.

A few more minutes of sitting like this and I might have to bail on this whole thing.

Five minutes later, I truly wished I hadn't relied on him for a ride. It was bad enough to be uncomfortable, but having to listen to seventies classic rock and not say a word threatened to make me go crazy.

Knowing I was breaking one of the cardinal rules of being in his car, I reached over and turned the music down. Without a word, Kane narrowed his eyes to angry slits. "Unless you're going to tell me you see him, there was no reason to turn that off."

I tilted my head to the left and right to crack my neck. "No, I don't see him, and I'm starting to go stir crazy sitting here in silence. Can't we at least have a conversation if we're going to be stuck doing this?"

Kane's eyes scanned the restaurant for a moment before he looked over at me. "What do you want to talk about, Stefan?"

Boredom had clearly settled into his brain too if he was willing to chat, but I didn't care. Anything was better than what I'd been suffering through for the past two hours.

"Well, for one thing, I'm wondering why you haven't told Abbi what's going on with this Sebastian guy. What's with all the cloak and dagger shit?"

The angry slits came back in response to my question, and then he gruffly answered, "What I tell my wife or don't tell my wife is none of your business."

"Great. Thanks for that scintillating conversation. It was thrilling."

I returned to staring out the window to spy some guy who supposedly looked the spitting image of the person I sat next to. All I could hope for was he had a better disposition. I didn't need another cranky brother. I had my fill of them already.

Another few minutes passed with no sight of the guy, so I looked over at Kane to see if he was as frustrated as I was. I saw nothing in his face to tell me he felt anything at all. Talk about a poker face.

"Maybe we should accept the fact that either he got past us somehow or John got his quitting time wrong. Not that this hasn't been great fun and all, but I think we're wasting our time."

Kane said nothing and remained stone-faced as he stared at the back door of the building. Unless I planned to have Shay drive out to get me, I was trapped there.

Swell.

Still focused on the restaurant, Kane finally said, "I haven't told Abbi for the same reason Cash doesn't want anything to do with this."

"Because you're worried this guy contacted you because he's a money grubber?"

He shook his head, and for one of the few times since we parked the car looked at me. "No, because I want to protect her and the kids. If Sebastian turns out to be some piece of shit who's going to bring nothing but bad into our lives, I don't want the people I love the most to have to deal with that. I'll deal with it on my own and they'll never have to know."

"I don't get you, Kane. You and Abbi have this love that transcends everything kind of relationship, yet you keep shit from her. Everyone looks and Shay and me like we're the lamest couple ever, yet I don't keep anything from her. I told her about this possible new brother the day you told me."

I knew I was treading on dangerous ground questioning his relationship with Abbi. Of all the things in his life, what he had with her was the most important of them all. I wasn't just being a bust ass when I described their love as the kind that transcends all. That was how he saw them. Everyone else was common and average compared to how he felt for her.

He didn't lash out at me, though. Actually, if anything, his expression and body language relaxed as he listened to me talk.

"Abbi and Shay are very different people, Stefan. Abbi relies on me to protect her. Shay doesn't need that from you."

Kane wasn't wrong about Shay. She was a fighter, no doubt. I liked that about her. But Abbi wasn't as delicate as my brother made her out to be. I'd seen her go toe-to-toe with him on more than one occasion, and she held her own, even as he towered over her glaring down at every word coming out of her mouth.

"I think you underestimate your wife, dude. She's not some dainty flower that is going to wilt at the first sign of bad times. Hell, last Fourth of July I thought she was going to slug you after you broke Cash's wrist arm wrestling. I think if Olivia hadn't freaked out, she would have torn you a new one."

Looking out the front window, he sighed. "It's not the same thing. That's harmless fun." A small smile turned up the corners of his mouth. "Well, harmless unless you're Cash."

Since I had him talking and I'd even gotten a rare smile from him, I asked what had been on my mind since hearing that Cash had just found out about the bad feelings between Abbi and Shay. "Hey, I'm curious. Why does your wife still dislike my girlfriend? I mean, that was years ago and nothing happened."

In a flash, everything about him iced over. "No idea."

If I was a suspicious man, I might have wondered what this sudden change in behavior was about. I knew Kane, though. His unwillingness to speculate on why Abbi continued to irrationally dislike Shay over one night years ago that didn't even involve them having sex was the result of some kind of guilt he still carried to that day.

Not that he shouldn't feel shitty about how he acted way back when. He should. It just seemed that the whole jealousy thing Abbi carried around should have a statute of limitations even if his guilt didn't.

I wanted to say that, but why bother? He'd either not respond at all or get pissed and take a swing at me.

After sitting there for hours bored out of my gourd, the last thing I wanted was a slugfest with the brother I had no chance of taking. If it was Cash, I might have at least entertained the idea. On off days, beating him was a definite possibility.

Then again, Cash would have never forced me to sit in some old car listening to goddamned golden oldies for hours while he remained sullen and silent staring out the window. At least with him I would have been sitting on some luxury seat.

Just then, Kane leaned forward toward the dash and pointed at someone walking out the back door of the restaurant. "Look."

I did as he said and saw a dark haired male leaving alone and walking toward a car on the far end of the parking lot. Well, staggering was a better description. The guy looked like his brain had forgotten how to put one foot in front of the other.

After a few seconds of watching his drunken ass stumble and seeing him nearly go head over heels over a curb, I wondered aloud, "Are we going to let this guy drive anywhere? He looks like he can barely walk, much less drive."

Kane made some noise that sounded like he was disgusted and opened his door to get out. "Stay here if you want. I don't think he's going to be much to handle in his state."

"What are you going to do with him?"

As he slammed the door, I heard him say, "I'm going to make sure he doesn't kill himself or someone else."

Confused as to why I just sat doing the incognito thing for hours if we were going to meet the damn guy face-to-face anyway, I jumped out of the car and jogged to catch up to Kane as he got to Sebastian, our potential new brother who currently was fall down drunk and lying on the pavement.

"Dude, he's fucked up," I said with a chuckle as we stood over him. "You're going to have to take him home."

The look on Kane's face told me this was way more than he'd signed up for when he picked me up tonight. As distasteful as it was to me too, we couldn't leave the guy in the shape he was in and risk him driving somewhere when he woke up. We'd have to get him home.

Hopefully, he wasn't so fucked up that he didn't know where he lived.

"You know, this could mean he's not one of Dad's. We handle our drink a little better than this."

Kane slowly turned his head and stared at me like I'd said something nonsensical. "Do I need to remind you of all the nights Cash or I or both of us had to mop you up off the floor at Club X in the early days? Man, you were a sloppy ass drunk when you were younger."

I wanted to disagree, but he wasn't wrong. I was

exactly how he described me. But by the time I was this guy's age, I had learned to drink better than he had, at least.

From the ground, Sebastian Thorne opened his eyes and looked up at us. "I don't have drink more money tonight so fuck off."

Staring down at him like he was some burden he hated, Kane said, "Help me get him up."

I reached for Sebastian's arm as Kane lifted his other side, but the guy seemed practically boneless and slid out of our holds, laughing as he hit the ground with all his weight. Looking down at his stupid ass lying there, all I knew was I definitely hadn't signed on to be some drunk's babysitter tonight.

Undaunted, Kane waved me on to grab his arm again. "Hold on to him this time, for fuck's sake. He's like dead weight."

I lifted Sebastian's right side, snapping back, "Which means you could do this all on your own."

Finally, we got him onto his feet and stable. Turning to look at me first and then Kane, Sebastian said, "Are you my…my uh…guardian angels?"

Kane simply glared at him, but since I was feeling particularly smart assed at that moment, I answered, "Yeah, that's it. We're angels. Now behave or I'm going to smack the fuck out of you with my wings."

CHAPTER SIX

KANE

SEBASTIAN SAT IN THE BACKSEAT of the Mustang, complaining the entire time as I drove toward his apartment about a dozen blocks from where he worked. Worried he'd throw up all over my car, I kept one eye on him and one eye on the road, regretting my choice to get a look at him tonight.

"So now we're some kind of drunk car service?" Stefan grumbled.

I didn't want to discuss this new turn of events with him, especially since he'd seen this night unraveling hours ago. Even he hadn't predicted this end, though.

"Uh, who are you guys?"

Telling Sebastian we may or may not have been his brothers didn't seem like the right thing to say, but other than that explanation, I had nothing but anger. I figured I'd let Stefan handle the guy since he seemed like he wanted to talk.

He turned to look into the backseat and said, "What's your fucking problem? Do you have short-term memory loss or something? I just told you five minutes ago who we are. Angels, remember?"

I watched in the rearview mirror as Sebastian grew even more confused. Finally, after he appeared to think through what he'd heard, he said, "Really? Like real angels?"

Stefan laughed like any of this was funny. "The stupid is strong with this one. I'm severely doubting he could be one of us."

"One of you? What are you guys, like some secret society? Are you taking me to your hideout?"

It was like babysitting a teenage boy with delusions of grandeur. Looking back at him, I asked, "Did you give me the right directions to your house back there?"

Slapping me in the shoulder, Stefan laughed. "I like this guy. He's dumb as a post, but he's funny as all hell."

"I have been told that I'm funny," Sebastian slurred.

"What's your fucking address?" I barked, startling him.

"My address? 745 Chest…Chestnuts. I mean, Chestnut. Yeah, that's it. My favorite nut. Chestnuts."

"I swear if that's not right, I'm going to pound the fuck out of him just on principle," I said to no one in particular, just needing to let off some steam before I reached back and slapped this guy silly.

"So how's that new brother thing working for you

now, Kane? Still pumped about the idea?" Stefan teased as I made a left turn onto Chestnut Street.

I looked at the numbers on each house hoping we were close. 700 block. Now I just had to find 745, unload him into his apartment, and go home to Abbi and the kids.

"Right now, I'm thinking being an only child might be a really great thing."

With a glance into the backseat, I saw Sebastian had fallen asleep. I elbowed Stefan and said, "Wake him up. We're almost there."

By the time I parked the car in front of the house, he was awake again and completely confused. While Stefan tried to explain what had happened, I turned the car off and announced to both of them it was time to get out, praying to God he'd given me the right address because if he hadn't, it was going to take every ounce of will power I possessed not to just leave him right there on Chestnut Street.

Sebastian stumbled out of the car and onto the sidewalk in typical drunk fashion, nearly landing on his face after less than three steps. It had been a long time since I had to babysit a drunk like this, and I didn't miss it. To be honest, Stefan had been a better time when he was hammered. This one was just sloppy.

We held him up for a few feet until we got to a set of steps leading to a narrow white house. Holding his arms out, Sebastian slurred, "I got this. I'm cool. I got it."

He put one foot on the first step and feel face forward, landing flat on the stairs to the porch. Jesus Christ, I was beginning to hate this guy. Brother or not, he was a pain in the ass. Stefan stood doubled over with laughter as Sebastian groaned in pain.

"Holy fuck, this guy is hysterical! Now I'm hoping he's our brother just for the laughs."

I'd had enough of this shit. Scooping the now bloody-faced Sebastian up, I threw him over my right shoulder and marched up to the door next to the number 745 on the house. With Stefan behind me, I knocked on the door but got no answer.

Nudging Sebastian, I asked, "Is the person you live with at home?"

He opened his blue eyes and nodded. "I don't know. Dani might not be here now. Get my key out of my pocket."

I looked over at Stefan. "You heard him. Time to go fish."

His expression twisted into a grimace. "I'm not sticking my hand in some guy's pants, Kane."

"I swear to God, Stefan, if you don't get those fucking keys, I'm going to use you and him as battering rams and bust this goddamned door down. Now get the keys."

In a flash, he changed his tune. Reaching into Sebastian's pocket, he mumbled, "Okay, okay. Man, you're so testy."

I regretted ever even thinking I should try to find out any more about this possible brother of ours at the moment, and testy wasn't even close to what I was really feeling. Enraged was more like it.

Stefan jingled a set of keys in front of him and smiled as he opened the front door to the house. "Open sesame. Easy peasy. No need to threaten anyone."

Before he could take the keys out of the doorknob, I pushed past him into a living room that looked like something out of a frat house. Beer bottles lay strewn around the room, with a few empty liquor bottles still standing on the coffee table in front of the couch. Fast food bags lay on the floor and on the chair in the corner. If any female lived there, I didn't want to meet her.

"Fuck, he's a pig," Stefan said as I dumped Sebastian onto the couch. "Dude, is this how you live?"

Sebastian opened his eyes and looked around like he didn't know where he was. "Dani must not have cleaned up before she and her friends left. That's what I get for letting her hang out here. Damn."

He made a move to grab one of the empty vodka bottles on the table but gave up or changed his mind and just sat back against the couch. Sure he was safe and not going to be driving anytime soon since his car was still back at the CocoNut parking lot, I motioned with my head to Stefan it was time to leave.

"But you wanted to get a look at the guy, so why don't we take the time to at least talk to him? He might be, you know, our brother."

"I already know too much about him," I said as I took a step toward the door.

Stefan grabbed my arm to stop me before I made it very far. "Come on. Just a couple minutes. We waited all those hours. What's a few minutes more?"

"If you're so eager to talk to him, go ahead. I'll just stay here next to the door. You have five minutes."

Undaunted by my lack of interest, Stefan jumped at the chance to find out more about the drunken mess of a person with a bloody nose who was barely keeping his eyes open. Positioning himself next to him on the couch, he said, "Hey, dude, wake up. Let's talk."

Sebastian's eyes opened wide and fixed on him. "I didn't realize you were still here. What do you want from me?"

"What's your deal? Do you always get stone drunk on a Monday night?"

I couldn't help but smile at the judgmental tone in Stefan's voice. It wasn't that many years ago that he got drunk every night of the week and Cash and I had to deal with him.

Scrubbing his face, Sebastian seemed to think about the questions for a minute. His voice a little less slurred, he said, "Well, not that it's any of your business, but I decided to have a few after work tonight with one of the girls who works at CocoNut's. So after Tawny got off, we got to drinking."

"I thought you said your girlfriend's name was Dani."

More judgment from someone who used to go through women like they were water.

Sebastian grinned and with a shrug said, "I didn't say she was my wife or anything. We hang out. Why do you fucking care? Who are you again?"

Before I could stop him, Stefan outed the both of us. "I'm Stefan and this is Kane."

Looking at each of us, he said, "I know those names. Did you tell me in the car?"

Hoping to lie well enough to confuse him, I spoke up. "Yeah, we did, but we have to go. Stef, let's go. Now."

He held his hand up to stop me. "Wait a minute. I want to talk more to Sebastian here. So did you get anywhere with that Tawny girl?"

I rolled my eyes. Of all the questions he could ask the guy, that was the one that came to his mind first? Maybe old Stefan wasn't entirely gone after all.

Sebastian nodded. "Yeah, I did. It was sort of like shooting fish in a barrel, though, I have to admit. She's wanted me for a while, so I figured why not, right? You're only young once, and I'm not tied down to anyone."

Stefan looked over at me and smiled. "I like this

guy. He's a shitty drunk, but I like his attitude. He reminds me of me a few years ago."

"Yeah. That's a reason to not like someone, Stef. Let's go."

Ignoring me, Stefan asked Sebastian, "So what else do you do other than work at a restaurant, get drunk, and pick up women?"

"Is there anything else to do around here?" Sebastian answered way too cocky. More and more, I started to believe he was another son of Cassian March.

"Well, no, probably not, but if you could do other things, what would you do?"

He ran his hands through his black hair and thought about the question for a few seconds. "I always dreamed of going west. You know, getting out of this state and seeing the rest of the country. I've never seen mountains, so I'd like to see them."

Time was up. "Stefan, come here."

Both of them looked at me, but thankfully Stefan didn't argue with me and came over to where I was standing. Shaking my head, I tried to find the words to make him understand I had no more interest in whatever he was trying to do with Sebastian.

"I'm not sure what this whole high school guidance counselor thing you have going on with this guy is, but your five minutes is up. Time to go."

I saw in his dark eyes he really wanted to know more about the guy. He had that curious look in them.

"Come on, Kane. I think he could be our brother. Don't you want a chance to get to know him a little?"

"No. He reminds me too much of what you were like in the early days at the club."

Stefan sneered. "Don't be an asshole. He's just a kid having a good time. Just because you've been this serious guy all your life doesn't mean everyone else has to be. Give him a chance. Just a few minutes more."

Leaning down so my face was no more than an inch away from his, I fixed my gaze on him. "I'm not interested in finding out any more about this guy."

He looked over at Sebastian lying back on the couch, his face still bloody. "At least let's clean him up a little. He's a mess. Give me a minute and then we can leave."

I watched as Stefan got a wet paper towel from the kitchen and handed him it. "You're bleeding, man. You know, from when you fell on the stairs. Use this on your face."

Confused, Sebastian asked, "I fell on the stairs? When?"

"Just take it and clean your nose. You might have broken it. At least it's stopped bleeding, though," Stefan said in his most helpful voice.

A knock at the door tore me away from the odd scene playing out in front of me, but before I opened it, I asked, "Any idea who this could be?"

I wasn't in the mood for any more bullshit tonight.

"It could be Dani or maybe Tawny. I guess it could be anybody," Sebastian said like he'd given up thinking about the correct answer after two names.

If this guy was our brother, the three of us had a responsibility as his big brothers to get rid of that idiotic way he had about him. And straighten his ass out with the drinking.

As long as it wasn't some guy on the other side of the door who wanted to finish what the stairs had started, I'd be happy. Whoever it was could come in and deal with him and Stefan and I could leave.

I liked that plan.

Turning the knob, I opened the door and stared out into the night to see not Dani or Tawny or anyone else I should see on Sebastian's porch.

Before I had the chance to say a word, the person who'd knocked glared up at me. I'd seen that look before, but I certainly hadn't expected to see it at that moment.

What the hell was Abbi doing at Sebastian's apartment?

CHAPTER SEVEN

ABBI

MY HEART SUNK AS I stared up at Kane standing there in the doorway to that house. Who lived there? Did the woman I'd suspected he'd been cheating on me with live there and he was spending time with her instead of at the restaurant fixing that electrical problem like he'd claimed hours earlier?

"Abbi, what are you doing here? Who's watching the kids?" he asked in a voice that teetered between angry and confused.

I tried to look around him, but he blocked my view. "Who's in there, Kane? Who is she? I can't believe you'd do this to us!"

He closed the door and began to guide me down the front steps toward the car. "Angel, you have this all wrong. Go home and I'll be back in less than an hour."

"I will not go home!" I angrily answered, pushing against him to get away so I could see who this woman was who he felt he should throw his life away for. The life we'd made together.

I flung the door open just as Kane caught my arm and saw Stefan sitting on the couch with another man. Looking around for the woman, I saw no one but them. Unsure what was going on, I pointed at Stefan and demanded, "Tell me where she is right now. I know she's here."

He said something about me being mistaken, but as he spoke I noticed the man sitting next to him was Sebastian, the man I'd had coffee with a few weeks ago after Alexandria had told me about her husband fathering another son the three brothers hadn't met yet.

"Sebastian? What are you doing here with them? And what happened to your face?"

I turned to look at Kane as he glared at him. "Did you hit him?"

"Abbi, right?" Sebastian said with a chuckle. "The girl from the coffee shop. I have no idea why all you people are in my apartment, but you're a nice addition."

Stefan looked back and forth between Kane and me and Sebastian with a thoroughly confused expression before finally saying, "How do you two know each other?"

From behind me, Kane said in a low, angry voice, "Exactly what I was about to ask."

I spun around and stared up at my husband, my arms folded across my chest to hold me back from lashing out. "So you think you're in a position to ask anything since you've been lying to my face for at least a week about where you've been going?"

Kane said nothing, but he didn't look away. Instead, he met my angry gaze with one of his own. Behind me, I heard Stefan say to Sebastian, "Oh, you're going to love these two! He routinely lies about things because he thinks she needs to be protected, and when she finds out about one, she goes toe-to-toe with him about it. It makes for some great family get-togethers, I can tell you."

Sebastian, still clearly confused, asked, "So are you his sister or something?"

I turned around to explain who I was, but Kane pushed me behind him and said flatly, "She's my wife, and you're about to tell me why you were having coffee with her."

Stefan jumped up from the couch. "Whoa, I know that look. I don't think this is what you think it is, Kane. Let the guy explain before you go pounding him into the ground."

Backing up to the far end of the couch, Sebastian put up his hands in surrender. "Dude, no need to go pounding anything on me. We weren't having coffee together. Well, we were, but it wasn't like it was a date or anything. She was just there at the coffee shop and asked me if she could sit down at the table I was at since it was so crowded. Nothing else. We had a nice talk for a few minutes. I swear that was it. Honest."

Kane took a step toward him, but I grabbed his arm to stop him. "He's telling the truth. Don't do anything."

For a moment, I wasn't sure he believed either of us. I knew my husband better than anyone else in the world, and hearing I was spending time with some man, even if I wanted to find out if he was his brother, wasn't something he ever wanted to hear.

To say he was possessive was an understatement.

He looked down at me with a mixture of hurt and anger in those dark blue eyes, and I knew he was struggling to not act on his nature. Hoping to convince him, I brought his left hand to my lips and pressed a soft kiss onto the wedding band that matched mine.

"I would never be with anyone else. You know that, Kane. My time with Sebastian at that coffee shop was mere coincidence. I was there to meet Gemma."

That my being at that coffee shop that day wasn't a coincidence at all wasn't anything he needed to know. At least not at that moment as Stefan and Sebastian sat there watching us.

Cradling my face, Kane said in a soft voice I knew was forced, "Abbi, I'll be home in a little while after I get finished here. We'll talk when I get home."

I didn't need to argue anything after he said that. There was no point. I knew my husband. I could either understand that he didn't want to talk about this there and cause a scene, which would result in him taking me to the car, or I could accept that he was trying to be what he'd always promised he'd be to me.

The kind of man I wanted.

True, he was jealous and possessive and he lied to me to protect me from things I didn't need protecting from, but beyond all that, he loved me like I was the queen of his world. I accepted the bad with him because of that good.

Without another word, I turned to leave, but Kane gently touched me on the shoulder to stop me. I looked back at him and saw a tiny smile that went all the way up to his eyes. Everything would be okay.

IT WAS MORE THAN AN hour later, but he finally returned home just after I got the kids tucked into their beds and read Annalea her nighttime story. Kane sat down on his side of the bed and silently slid out of his shirt before turning to look at me.

"It wasn't a coincidence that you were at that coffee shop, was it?" he asked in a low voice.

Caught off guard by how direct his question was, I took a deep breath. There was no point in lying. I wasn't ashamed of anything I'd done.

"No."

He studied my face for a moment before he spoke again. "You went there to meet him because you think he's my brother?"

"Yes. Alexandria told me the story a few weeks ago,

and I wanted to see for myself. So I found out where he works and followed him to that coffee shop."

Kane sighed and hung his head. "Why? You could have been hurt. What if he was some guy who kidnaps and rapes women?"

I reached over to touch his shoulder. "I'm not some virginal girl who doesn't know a thing or two about bad men. I haven't always been with you. I was smart about it. I caught up with him in a public place in broad daylight. I was never in any danger, baby."

Kane turned his head to face me, and I saw the worry in his eyes. "I remember, Abbi. I've spent every minute of my life with you making sure you don't have to, though."

"I know you want to protect me. I get that. It's who you are, and I love you for it. No woman has a more wonderful or more protective husband than I do. It's just that I'm not some naïve child who needs to be shielded from things, Kane. I'm a grown woman and your wife, but sometimes it feels like you treat me like one of the kids."

He closed his eyes and leaned back on the bed so his head was in my lap. When he opened them, he nodded. "I just want to be the kind of man for you that my mother never had. She worried about everything, and it made her bitter and hateful to my father. I don't want you to ever have to worry."

"I love that you want to be that for me, baby," I

said as I ran my fingers through his soft, black hair, longer now than when we first met. "I just wish you could see that I can be more than someone you have to protect. You can share things with me. Even bad things, Kane, because when you don't and you keep them from me, I end up worrying anyway."

He thought about what I said for a minute and smiled before sitting up to face me. "Did you tell him you thought he was our brother?"

Shaking my head, I thought about my brief encounter with Sebastian at the coffee shop near his house and chuckled. "No. I never planned to do that. I just wanted to see for myself if he could be another son of Cassian March. He looks the part, but other than that, all I found out was he's a little like I imagine Stefan would be if he was single. Definitely a player."

A serious look came over Kane's face. "Did he hit on you?"

"No, not so much hit on me. I got the feeling he doesn't see anyone out of his reach, though."

Relieved to hear Sebastian hadn't tried to get into my pants, Kane nodded in agreement with my description of the guy's attitude toward women. "He's definitely cocky."

"So do you think he's your brother?"

"I don't know. He looks a lot like me and Cash, but so far my guy hasn't found out anything that proves he's another son."

"Now that you've met him, do you want him to be?"

Kane's eyebrows rose. "The jury's still out on that."

I leaned over and kissed his cheek. "Do you know why I wanted to see if he was another son of your father's?"

"No. Did Alexandria make it seem like it was important to find him?" Kane asked, clearly in the dark about why I would bother to search out this person.

"No, I did it because he'd be like you. From what she said, he never really knew his father either. I just thought if you knew someone was out there who was like you in that way that you'd want to know about him."

Kane kissed me softly on the lips in that way he did when he wanted me to know how much he loved me without saying it. "If you know me so well, how could you think I'd ever cheat on you, Abbi?"

I hated that I'd been so stupid to think that this man who gave me everything he was without hesitation would go with anyone else. Deep in my heart I knew he wouldn't, but my insecurities had gotten the better of me.

"I knew you weren't telling me the truth. When you lie to protect me, I can't help it. I think it's because you're doing things with someone else."

He looked at me in that pained way that showed how much he hated hurting me and kissed me again.

"I'm sorry. I don't mean to make you doubt me. I just didn't want to bring him into our lives until I found out if he was really our brother and I knew he was the kind of person I want around the woman I love and my children."

I laid my head on his shoulder, loving the strength he offered just by being there to protect me. "For nearly seven years, I've tried to show you that I can handle being with you. You deserve a wife who you can tell things to, not some delicate soul you always feel like you have to watch over and protect. I'm not that girl I was when you met me anymore. I love that you want to keep me and the kids safe, but I'd love it even more if you included me in things like this."

I knew I was asking him to be different than he naturally was. I also knew he'd never truly be like Cash was with Olivia. It simply wasn't who he was.

Kane swallowed hard and looked down at the bed. "I hide things so you don't get hurt, but even more, so you aren't in danger. I don't know what I'd do if I lost you, angel."

"You aren't going to lose me. I found the best man in the world, Kane. I'm not going to let this life we have go for anything."

He smiled at me and nodded. "From now on, when my brothers and I get together to talk about this, I'd like you to be there. I should mention that it might mean Shay will be around because Stefan told her everything."

A tiny lick of jealousy flared inside me every time Kane even said her name. I knew it was stupid and irrational because they'd both sworn nothing ever happened between them, but that had never been the problem. She'd been the one to convince him to be there for me and Annalea, not me.

I wasn't jealous that he cared for her. I was jealous still all these years later that my words hadn't been enough but hers had.

Forcing a smile, I kissed him. "That's fine. What about Olivia and Cash?"

Kane shrugged. "So far they don't want any part of this new brother thing. I guess I don't blame them. If Cash had seen him tonight, I don't think that would have helped either. He seems to be nothing more than a fall down drunken kid of twenty-six."

"Well, whatever he is, if he's your brother, you're going to have to decide how much you want to do with him."

Bringing my hand to his mouth, Kane kissed my wedding band and smiled. "We're going to have to decide."

It wasn't a huge step, but it was a step, nonetheless. Knowing Kane, that word we're meant the world to me.

Chapter Eight

Cassian

MY PHONE BUZZED AS I pulled my car into my parking spot behind CK. Looking down at where it sat in the console, I saw it was Stefan. To get a call from that brother before noon was like seeing snow for the Fourth of July, so I quickly answered it, curious as to what had gotten him out of bed so early.

"Hey, Stef. What's up?"

"Have you talked to Kane yet today?" he asked hurriedly, like he hoped I hadn't so he could tell me what he had to say.

Turning the engine off, I slid out of the driver's seat and slammed the door. "No, why?"

"You missed a good time last night. Well, not the first few hours, but the last one was much better."

Struck by how unlikely those words were coming from Stef about a night out with Kane, I stopped dead at the back door to the building. "You two went out last night? Really?"

Stefan's laughter at even the suggestion came

through loud and clear. "Uh, no. We might not hate each other, but Kane and I have completely different ideas of what constitutes a good time. No, we went on a stakeout. Well, sort of a stakeout."

I could imagine this brother doing something like that, but Kane? He was the steady rock among the three of us, and now he was going on stakeouts with Stefan? And why would either of them be part of a stakeout? What the hell was going on?

As I opened the back door to the restaurant, I said, "I'm not sure I even want to ask what you mean, but I am curious why Kane of all people would be doing something like that, and with you, to boot."

Sounding like I'd hurt his feelings, Stefan asked, "Why be like that? Kane and I get along fine. We have for a while. We even do things together."

Now it was my turn to laugh. "Really? Since your girlfriend and his wife can't be in the same place for more than a few seconds, exactly what are you doing together?"

"So now that you finally caught up with the rest of us this is going to be part of every damn conversation with you? And unlike you, Cash, we can do things without our women tagging along. Seriously, dude, when did you become so whipped?"

I dropped my keys onto my desk and shut the door to my office. "It's not being whipped if you really love the person, Stef. So are you going to tell me what you and Kane did that you called me about this morning or are we just going to continue with the insults about my happiness?"

Stefan sighed like he was six years old again and I'd just popped his balloon. "Jeez, everybody in this family is so fucking testy."

"It's just that I have a busy day ahead of me and need to get going with work."

In truth, I had a sinking feeling the story he was about to tell me had to do with Sebastian and the possibility he was our brother, something I didn't want to think about at that moment. Or any other moment in the foreseeable future. Kane and Stef may have been all jacked up about getting a new baby brother, but I didn't want to be involved.

"Fine. I'll make it short then," Stefan said in his hurt feelings voice. "We ended up meeting Sebastian Thorne last night and it was going pretty well until Abbi showed up and Kane thought she'd been with the guy. Well, I don't know about well because he was pretty drunk, but he's definitely a good time. We still don't have any real proof that he's one of us, but he damn sure looks like it. He's the spitting image of Kane."

Whatever he said after Abbi being with the guy who might be our brother got lost in the recesses of my mind. Confused, I said, "Wait a second. Abbi and Sebastian Thorne know each other? Before or after she met Kane?"

What the hell was I saying before or after? Abbi wasn't the type of woman to cheat on anyone, and for God's sake, she adored Kane. Maybe I'd heard Stefan wrong.

"No, no. Abbi met him just a month or so ago. Odd coincidence, I guess. But that's not the point of the story. Keep up, Cash. The point is we met him and got to talk to him face-to-face. I have to say I'm definitely hoping he's one of us now."

"Why? Because he's a good time?"

The phone fell silent for a moment, and then Stefan said, "Well, yeah. It's hard being the only person in our family who still knows how to have fun. Marriage has ruined you, and Kane has been a lost cause since the night he met Abbi. It'll be nice to have someone around who isn't all about work and home for a change."

Sometimes Stefan was still that twenty-one year old punk ass brother who refused to see that life was more than drinking too much and screwing women. I'd hoped Shay would help that, but even after all these years together, she and he seemed no closer to settling down. That only encouraged him to think he could still act like a kid.

"Well, that's nice for you, Stef. I'm a little busy today, so have fun," I said as I opened my laptop to begin my day.

"That's it? You're still not even the least bit interested in finding out anything about this guy who very well might be our brother? I mean, what the fuck, Cash?"

"Stef, by the way you've made him sound, I can't imagine having anything in common with this Sebastian person. I'm just a boring guy running a successful business and loving my family. I'll leave you to find out about him, and if he's in fact our brother, I'm sure I'll meet him at some family get-together at some point."

I couldn't imagine that ever really happening, in truth. While my mother had accepted Kane, I doubted she'd be inviting yet another of my father's kids over for the next family barbeque. Then again, she did love Stefan and nothing made her happier than to encourage him on his flights of fancy, so maybe she would welcome another illegitimate son with open arms.

Regardless, I wanted nothing to do with the whole damn matter. Our father's sexual peccadillos and the results of them weren't anything I had room for in my world. If Stefan and Kane cared, so be it.

It didn't change how I felt.

"So you still don't want to find out about him?"

"Nope. You and Kane can have at it."

Stefan grunted. "So is Kane in yet? I'm curious to know how he's doing this morning."

"No. If you want to talk to him, you'll have to find him at home, I'm guessing. You know, where his wife and kids are, the people he lives for."

More grunting came through the phone. "Whatever. Nice talking to you, Cash."

"Same here, Stef. Talk to you later."

I tossed my phone onto the pile of papers on the corner of my desk and tried to push the thought of brothers entirely out of my mind. I knew Stefan wouldn't let up on this whole Sebastian issue, though. It had become like a cause to him, and when my younger brother found something to focus on, there was no changing his mind.

That was fine, but I didn't want to think about it anymore. I'd heard whispers about my father's other kids all my life, and I was sick of it. Maybe that was selfish of me because I'd had the luck of being his firstborn and namesake, but I didn't care.

I'd done everything my father had ever asked of me without question. I'd lived my life so he could be proud. To the day he died, I looked up to him.

But now that I was a husband and father myself, I could see the chinks in his armor. The man I'd idolized all those years hadn't been good to my mother or his children by her. Stefan still bore the emotional scars of being overlooked his entire life by the one man he wanted to notice him.

And me? I'd thought being like my father was

something to be proud of until I met Olivia. That my father had never come to that revelation for my mother ate at me every time I thought about him out fucking other women and producing kids all over town.

I loved Kane as much as I loved Stefan, but now that I had a wife and son of my own, I didn't want to have to keep welcoming my father's sins into my life anymore. This Sebastian person might very well be a great guy. He might be, but there was no room in the world I'd created for him and the baggage he undoubtedly would bring with him.

A knock on my office door tore me out of my thoughts, and I called out for whoever it was to come in. Kane appeared in my doorway dressed in his usual suit pants, dress shirt, and tie but looking unusually happy, especially considering what Stefan had told me about the events of the night before.

"You're in early this morning. It's not even eleven yet. What's up?"

His smile faded just a bit, and he said, "Wanted to make sure I took care of that issue with the produce people, so I got here early to talk to the owner. I'm tired of us getting only half of what we order and then having to listen to excuses. Plus, I needed to have a talk with Gabriel about the problems we had on Saturday."

"I'm glad it was you who met with him. I have to say I didn't want to be the one to do it," I admitted. "For a chef, he's way too emotional. I thought he was going to lose his mind the other day."

Kane folded his arms across his chest and leaned against the doorframe. "Well, I smoothed things over, so hopefully he's happier now. We can't afford to lose him, Cash. He's one of the reasons people come to this place."

"I know. I don't deny how good he is. I just don't like all the bullshit he brings into my work life."

Smiling, Kane nodded. "You're all about keeping the bullshit out it seems these days. Everything okay?"

I knew where he was going with this. "Yeah. I just prefer an uncluttered life filled only with this place and my family."

"And if Sebastian Thorne turns out to be our brother, will that include him?"

Usually I preferred Kane's way of being straight-forward. Today I would have liked him to be less frank, though, so I could pretend to not understand his meaning and escape more discussion of this damn Sebastian person.

I took a deep breath and let it out slowly, hoping if I chose my words correctly that I could avoid this discussion again in the future. "You and Stefan seem to have a one-track mind when it comes to that topic. I'm sorry, Kane, but I don't feel the same way you two do, so whatever happens with him, I'm not sure I'm ever going to be interested in being a part of it."

Wincing, Kane nodded again, and a look of

acceptance came over his face. "I get it. I just wanted to see if anything had changed in your mind. I won't ask again."

"Thanks. Now if you could convince Stefan to do the same."

Kane's smile returned, brightening his face. Chuckling, he said, "I don't see that happening. He loves the idea of having a younger brother who's more like him than we are."

I rolled my eyes, remembering my conversation with him. "I heard all about it. It sounds like he's found a potential partner in crime for his nights out. Shay's going to love that."

Knocking his knuckles off the door, Kane smiled. "Maybe. Well, I'll see you later. I've got a few errands to run before we open. Call me if you need me."

With that, he was gone. This was why we got along so well. If it was Stefan standing in my doorway, I'd be talking myself to death about this Sebastian thing until the restaurant opened.

And somehow I was supposed to want another brother just like him?

I OPENED THE DOOR TO our condo as silently as possible, knowing that Olivia had likely just gotten Cassian to sleep. A tired mother wanted nothing less than to have some idiot loping into the house at nearly midnight and waking up the child she'd spent hours finally getting into bed.

Even if that idiot was the man who loved her.

She sat curled up on the couch, her eyes closed as the TV played some movie we'd said we wanted to see over a year ago. We'd never gotten to the theater for that one or half a dozen others that had seemed interesting.

I leaned over and kissed her gently on the lips, waking her. She sat up with a start and shook the sleep from her head.

"Hey, did you just get home?" she whispered.

"Yeah. It was a late one tonight. How was your day?" I asked as I sat down next to her.

"Busy. Your son got into the flour and dumped the bag all over him. He looked like a little pasty ghost, and you should have seen the tub after I got him all clean. It looked like there had been a disaster in there. That took up about two hours of my day."

I pressed a kiss onto her forehead and held her tired body to mine. "I'll trade you. I'll take care of Cassian and you can deal with my brothers and this Sebastian nonsense."

Olivia squeezed me to her and whispered, "You still don't want anything to do with that? I know they want you to get on board."

Shaking my head, I closed my eyes and savored the feel of my wife next to me for the first time in over twelve hours. "No. All I want is right here and in his bedroom dreaming of the next disaster he has in store for us."

She didn't say anything else and with a heavy sigh drifted off to sleep in my arms. I didn't need another brother. I already had all I needed.

Chapter Nine

Kane

JOHN SAT IN THE SAME position where I'd left him two days before behind his old desk staring at his laptop. Wondering if he'd even left to get a bite to eat, I joked, "If all this job entails is sitting and surfing through porn, I think I found a new career."

He looked up at me as I leaned against the doorframe and sneered. "You wish. Take a seat."

I considered mentioning how I'd staked out Sebastian's workplace the other night, but I had the feeling John wasn't in the mood for jokes this afternoon.

"So what's so urgent that I needed to get down here ASAP?" I asked as I sat down in front of him. "Those were your exact words, weren't they?"

My question earned me another sneer. "You know, sometimes you're too much like that younger brother of yours, and that's not a compliment."

Never a big fan of Stefan's, John had more than once butted heads with him on jobs for Club X. My brother's lack of respect for the job of PI and his bragging that anyone with an internet connection and the ability to use Google could do what John did pissed him off. Not that I blamed him. Stefan's bragging had brought me to the brink of giving him a good beating more than once.

"Sorry. I didn't mean to step on your toes with my joking. I'm just in a good mood today," I said, genuinely hoping to smooth over his hurt feelings. A good PI like John was worth his weight in gold. I didn't want to lose him because I felt like busting ass.

His angry expression softened a bit, and he seemed to study my face for a moment before asking, "Oh yeah? That's not like you, Kane, so what's up?"

"Nothing. Just happy at home and happy at work. What more could a man ask for?"

John looked around his dingy office and forced a smile. "I know just what you mean. Living the dream."

He didn't go into it, but I had a feeling his life was anything but a dream since his wife left. Quickly, I changed the subject. "So what's going on? Did you find out something about Sebastian Thorne?"

Nodding, he said, "I did, and I hate to ruin your good day, but I don't think you're going to like what I have to tell you."

I thought back to the hour or so I'd spent with Sebastian and had to admit I wasn't sure I'd be that unhappy at hearing the news that he wasn't another of my father's sons. I imagined Stefan would be disappointed, though.

"Did you find out he's not related to me?"

John shook his head. "No, he is. I mean, you couldn't tell that just by looking at him? By the way, I have to say whatever you and Stefan thought you were doing was the textbook definition of not slick, my friend. I was sitting in my car watching the whole thing. It had a real meta feeling to it, you know?"

I hung my head to hide my embarrassment. "I hadn't planned on approaching him, but you saw how fucked up he was. I couldn't let him just drive away like that. He might have killed someone."

"You used to be part owner of a bar, weren't you? How did you do that job and drive home all the drunks every night?" he asked, busting my balls now.

"Funny. If you remember, I didn't deal with the bar part. I dealt with the fantasy and sex part. No need to drive guys home because they didn't get off."

A smile crept onto John's face. "Oh, the good old days. Not that I don't love your swordfish at CK, but I think I miss the perks of working for you when you owned Club X."

My PI had enjoyed the offerings on my floor of the club a number of times and always left a happy man. Of course, that might have been a contributing factor in why his wife left him for another guy.

"Well, we had to grow up someday. That life

skirting the law could only last so long. We all knew Club X had an expiration date."

John's eyes grew wide. "About that. Seems it might be in the March family DNA to want to walk that fine line with the cops. Your newest sibling's hands are a bit dirty."

This was why I had kept everything about Sebastian away from Abbi and the kids and why I suspected Cash wanted nothing to do with finding some long lost brother of ours. Neither of us cared how hypocritical it seemed for the two former owners of a fantasy club to have no interest in getting into anything that had even the hint of legal problems.

Having a wife and kids you adored did that to a man.

A sick feeling settled into my stomach. I didn't want to discard Sebastian because he was my brother, and there was dirty and then there was really dirty. I hoped he wasn't the latter.

"So what are we talking about here, John? A DUI or he likes to get high sometimes? Or something else?"

With a look that made it seem like he shared my sick feeling, John grimaced. "Something else. Stupid twenty-something tricks or smoking a little weed wouldn't make my face look like it does. No, he's got himself involved in something a little worse. I don't know all the details, but from what I can see, he and his friends are thieves. I'm guessing that's how he affords to rent a house on a cook's income."

"Thieves? Like knocking over gas station kind of thieves?" I asked, already hating how this was sounding.

John chuckled. "No, he's a little higher class than that. He and buddies stick to houses. A little B and E here and there can pay for a lot of stuff. I watched him and two friends hit one two nights ago."

"Fuck. I had hoped the fall-down drunk act was the worst of him."

"I'm guessing one of them poses as a pool guy or something so he can find a way in, and then when the coast is clear, he lets his friends in and they grab whatever they can before disappearing. The people who own the house come home to find they've been burgled and then later realize they don't have a pool boy or a gardener or whatever anymore. It's just clever enough to work for a few months, but he's going to get caught and soon. If I can watch them pull a job, it won't be long before the cops are onto them."

I hated to admit it, but Cash had been right all along. I didn't want to give up on Sebastian, though. I knew what his life had been, no matter what the circumstances of it were. Growing up not knowing your father or knowing you had brothers wasn't something he should have gone through. I lived it and it sucked. Maybe if we'd been around, he wouldn't have gotten into stealing from people.

Or maybe he was just a rotten fucker, even though

he came from the same father the three of us did.

"Do you want me to continue with this, Kane, or are you cutting your losses right here?" John asked, interrupting my thoughts about what type of person Sebastian Thorne really was.

I wasn't ready to walk away from him just yet. Standing, I said, "Keep on it for a little while longer. See what you can find out. Send me all the legal info, though. I want to know the details about who his mother is and those kinds of things, okay?"

"Sure. I'll get it all together and send it over later. Want me to send it to the restaurant, as usual?"

I thought back to what I'd said to Abbi last night about involving her in this whole Sebastian thing, but things had changed. Knowing the way he lived his life could potentially hurt my family made it impossible to have her with me on this.

I'd just have to make her understand why I had to do things this way if she found out.

CALLING STEFAN SHOULD HAVE BEEN on my plan for the rest of the afternoon. I knew he'd want in on anything having to do with Sebastian, regardless of what I found out from John about his extracurricular activities. But as much as Stefan wanted to know our new brother, I felt like I needed to go this alone until I found out how far gone the guy was.

Even more, though, was the truth that Stefan had

never had to know. He may not have had the relationship he wanted with our father, but he never doubted that he was Cassian March's son a day in his life. He had no idea what the world felt like without that security.

Whatever else Sebastian was, he and I were alike in that. And to me, that was enough to make him worth more than just one bad, drunken night and a negative report from John.

After driving by CocoNut's and not finding him there, I drove to his apartment and saw the car we'd seen in the parking lot. I wasn't sure what I wanted to say to him or even what I was doing there, but hearing he was involved in something that would eventually get him sent to jail awakened some older brother feelings I'd never experienced before.

I knocked on the front door and when he opened it, I couldn't help see the similarity in how we looked. Except for a few minor differences, he was a younger version of me. As I stood there staring at him, I wondered if that's what my son would look like years from now.

Pushing all the sentimentality out of my head for the moment, I said, "Can I come in?"

He looked me up and down and smiled. "You know, now that I'm sober, it's pretty hard to miss."

"What?"

"We could be twins. Well, if you weren't like ten

years older than me. My brothers and sisters don't even look as much like me as you do. It's freaking me out a little, to be honest. I'm sort of wondering if you're me come from the future to tell me something that's going to save my life."

"Not exactly, but how about you let me in and we talk?" I asked as I stepped toward him.

"You sure? You move pretty much the same as I do too."

It was hard not to like him, even though he had a stupid sense of humor. "Trust me. I'm not from the goddamned future, okay?"

Sebastian stepped aside to let me in and closed the door behind me. "Well, if you are, do me, I mean us, a favor and tell me who wins the next few Super Bowls and World Series because I think we should make some money off this whole thing. Since you're future me, you'll benefit too."

I turned to face him and looked directly into his dark blue eyes. "I'm not from the future. Enough with the jokes. I want to talk to you about something."

Shrugging, he plopped down into the chair and extended his arm to offer me a seat on the couch. "Well, since you aren't future me that can only mean one of two things. You're either my father or we have the same father."

His father? How old did this kid think I was?

"What do you know about your father, who I'm

not, obviously?"

He shrugged again. "Not much. My mother said I looked like him, not that I think she knew him all too well. I got the feeling I was the result of a one night stand, but I don't know for sure. Doesn't really matter because here I am anyway. So we share the same baby daddy?"

"Yeah, and if you can never call him that again, that would be great. We're brothers, along with the guy I was here with the other night and another one you haven't met yet."

"So? What does that mean?"

Christ, he reminded me of myself a few years back. If someone had come to me and announced he was my brother, I would have told him to go fuck himself and don't let the door hit him on his way out. As he sat there looking at me with an expression that told me he was completely unimpressed by the news I'd just told him, I couldn't help but be thankful he wasn't more like who I used to be.

"Well, what do you want it to mean?"

Sebastian twisted his face for a moment and said, "I don't know. No offense, dude, but you're a stranger to me. I get the feeling you care about me being your brother, but since this is all new to me, I can't honestly say I feel the same."

"Fair enough. I'm not here to invite you to Sunday dinner with a whole bunch of people you don't know. I just wanted to let you know who you come from and that there are three other people like you."

He took a deep breath and sighed. "Okay. I guess since you obviously know more than I do about our father maybe you can tell me about him. What was he like? Was he the kind of guy who let you sit on his lap and read you stories or more of a badass kind of guy?"

Too bad I didn't know the answer to his question. Not a good start, for sure.

"Well, I didn't exactly know him growing up either."

Sebastian looked unimpressed by my answer. "I guess this guy got around. Four sons and he didn't know either of us. Did he know the guy from the other night?"

"Yeah. He and the other one were his sons by his wife."

"So three different mothers of four of us. Nice. Dad was a player. I'm guessing then he looked like us. No wonder he got so much ass."

Damn, he was cocky.

I'd had enough of talking about our father and his sexual behavior. As much as I wanted Sebastian to feel like he had someone in me he could consider a brother, I was more concerned with trying to convince him to give up the stealing.

Unsure how to bring it up, I went with what came naturally. "I know what you're up to and how you're making money, and it isn't working at that restaurant."

His eyes widened for a moment, showing his surprise at my quick change of topic, but without missing a beat he said, "Oh yeah? You going to go all big brother on me and tell me I shouldn't be doing that?"

There was that cockiness again. Well, he wasn't the only one who could play that game. "Yeah, I am. If I could find out about it with little effort, then you aren't as slick as you think you are. You and your friends are going to get your asses thrown in jail if you don't stop."

He stood up and walked over to the door. Opening it, he said, "Don't let it hit you on your way out, big brother."

"I'm trying to help you here. Trust me. The mistakes you make today aren't the kind you want following you for the rest of your life, and spending a few years in jail will follow you."

"You know, that other guy told me a little about you guys that night, and it seems like the pot calling the kettle black when you sit here telling me about being worried I'm going to get in trouble. You guys ran an illegal club when you were my age. That seems a whole lot worse than grabbing some stuff from a few houses. I'm not sure you have the moral high ground here."

Before I got the chance to try to explain how different the two circumstances were, I heard someone outside yell, "Thorne! I told you last time if you cheated me again I'd be coming for my due. Time to pay up!"

Sebastian slammed the door and locked it. "It's been great talking to you, dude, but I'd suggest you get the hell out of here. Use the window."

"What?"

He began to explain something about the guy outside being a former partner in his little heist scheme, but the banging on the door made it hard to get the whole story. Not that it mattered. I had a feeling what I'd been warning Sebastian about a few seconds ago was about to come true right in front of me.

I looked over at the window and knew I should go out that way and leave him to his just desserts. The problem was I had just told him I was his brother, and what kind of brother would I be if I left him there to get his ass kicked?

Even if he deserved it.

"Just open the door. I'm sure we can talk this out, but on the off chance we can't, don't talk too much so you don't piss the guy off."

He did as I told him to and his former partner marched into his living room demanding the money he was owed. Ignoring everything I told him, Sebastian began rambling on with a boatload of bullshit even I knew was lies. The guy, a skinny blond kid who hadn't even grown to six foot and had wild eyes, shook his head rapidly, obviously unhappy with every word he was hearing.

"Shut the fuck up, Sebastian! You owe me, and I'm going to get my money now!"

"It's not like that, Rick. We weren't cheating you out of anything. It just takes time to cash in the goods. We have to be careful. And the reason we didn't include you in on the other night was because we thought you were busy with your girlfriend. We didn't want to cause you any more hassles."

For a moment, it looked like Rick wanted to believe what was coming out of Sebastian's mouth, but after the words filtered through his brain, it was clear he wasn't buying the bullshit line he was being fed.

He pulled a gun from behind his back and pointed it straight at Sebastian's head. "The money. Now."

Terrified, Sebastian put his hands up in front of him and backed away toward me. "Whoa, whoa! Rick! Dude, I don't have it. I can get it for you, but I don't have it right now. Just give me a couple days."

His begging had no effect on Rick, who continued to point the gun at his head. "Now. The whole amount or the last thing you steal is a look at me shooting you."

Sebastian looked over at me and silently asked for help, so I calmly asked, "How much does he owe you, Rick? Maybe I have it so we can settle all this right now."

He stared at me in confusion like he hadn't noticed

I was in the room until that very moment. "Two grand."

I knew I didn't have that kind of money on me, but maybe the five hundred or so I had in my wallet would pacify him enough to make him put the gun away. Hoping it would, I reached into my back pocket to get my money and then in a flash the gun went off.

Chapter Ten

Abbi

No matter how fast I drove, I felt like I wasn't going to reach the hospital in time. Over and over, the words the man said echoed in my head.

"Mrs. Jackson, there's been an accident. Your husband is en route to Lakeland General. He's been shot."

My heart raced as my brain fixed on the last word the officer had said. *Shot.* Kane had been shot.

I hadn't waited for him to tell me anything else. Nothing he could say would make me feel any better, so I hung up and quickly put Liam into the car as I called the one person I knew could help no matter what. I didn't know what else to do. I had to get to Kane before it was too late.

Tears rolled down my face as I tore up the road. What if I didn't get to him in time? The last words I'd said to him that morning were so meaningless. Have a good day. It's what I said to him every morning when he left the house for work. Worthless words I'd gotten so used to mindlessly repeating, like asking someone how they are when you don't really care.

I didn't want those to be the last words I ever said to the man who'd given me nearly seven of the happiest years of my life. I needed to tell him how much I loved him. I needed him to know that no matter what, I loved him more every day. That just the thought of him gone from my life made my chest ache from emptiness.

That I didn't know how I'd go on without him.

My phone rang, and I answered it, barely able to speak through my sobs. Alexandria's sweet voice said, "Abbi, I'll be at the hospital in just a few minutes. I'll take care of Liam and get Annalea from school so I can take them back to my house. I called Stefan and Cassian, and they're on their way too. Honey, I want you to stay positive, okay? Kane is strong and he's not going to give up on you and those two babies."

As tears blurred my eyes, I turned right into the hospital parking lot. "What if he's not strong enough, Alexandria? I don't know what I'm going to do if he..."

I couldn't finish that sentence.

"He is. Of all my sons, he's the strongest. He's had to be."

The memory of all Kane had gone through growing up and how much he'd suffered made me even sadder. After all that, to be taken now that he'd found real happiness as a father was unfair. I couldn't bear to think of it.

"I'm here now," I said as I jammed the car into park and jumped out to get Liam from his car seat.

"I'll be there in a few minutes, honey. Don't give up on him yet, Abbi. Don't."

THE EMERGENCY ROOM DOCTOR'S WORDS hit my ears but got lost in the haze of sorrow that had taken over my brain. I held Liam tightly to me, desperate for some piece of Kane to stay with me as the man in front of me said things about gunshot wounds and surgery to remove the bullet from his chest.

Gently, he touched my shoulder and gave me a sad smile. "As soon as he's out of surgery, we'll let you know, Mrs. Jackson."

I took a step back and felt the plastic seat of a waiting room chair hit the back of my knees. Sitting down, I tried to understand how any of this had happened. Where had Kane been at one o'clock in the afternoon? I had just gotten a text from him a few hours earlier telling me he'd be busy all day but he couldn't wait to see me when he got home. What had he been busy doing that got him shot?

Liam cooed in my arms and tugged at the bottom of my hair, so I looked down and pressed a smile onto my face. He had no idea of the nightmare we'd been thrust into.

"What's Mommy's little guy want? Grandma's

coming any minute, honey, and you're going to take a little ride with her back to her house with Annalea. I promise Mommy will come just as soon as she can."

I stared into my son's dark blue eyes so similar to his father's and struggled to hold back the tears. The spitting image of Kane, he seemed to sense I needed him to be an angel and simply smiled up at me, nearly breaking my heart. What if Kane never had the chance to see his son grow up? What if he never saw that precious smile again?

Alexandria arrived and sat down, wrapping her arms around me. The fear of losing Kane was written all over her face. "Oh, honey. Did you talk to the doctors? What did they say?"

Holding back the tears as best as I could, I told her what the doctor had told me. "We won't know anything until he's out of surgery. He was shot in the chest, Alexandria. What if it got his heart?"

Just saying those words made my tears come, and they began rolling down my cheeks. Burying my face in Liam's shoulder, I sobbed, "I don't know what I'm going to do."

"No more talking like that, Abbi. I told you. Kane is strong. A single bullet isn't going to take him from you and those beautiful babies."

Liam's tiny fingers gripped my neck, holding me to him, and I remembered the first time he clutched Kane's hand as a newborn. He'd joked about him having a tough grip, and I'd reminded him that he was only three weeks old. Kane had fallen in love with him the moment the nurse placed him in his arms minutes after he was born. Unlike with Annalea, he was full term and healthy as a horse, crying like he had the lungs of a grown man as he lay in his father's arms for the first time. I'd never forget how happy Kane had been at that moment.

I wanted the chance to see him that happy again.

And now he lay on an operating table with a bullet in his chest, fighting for his life, but why? What had happened?

I lifted my head and saw Alexandria's eyes full of sadness. "Why would anyone do this? Why wasn't he at work?"

She shook her head like she didn't know what to say. "I don't know, honey. I'm hoping maybe Cassian will be able to tell us something when he gets here."

"Did he know why Kane wasn't at the restaurant?"

"No. He was as shocked as I was when he heard what happened."

I sat there as Liam played with my hair and thought about how sure Kane had been that this kind of thing was behind us once he left Club X. "We're boring married people with kids now, angel. All that is in the past," he'd say when I worried about him leaving CK late at night.

How could I know the danger wouldn't be in the

dark as he walked to his car but in broad daylight on a sunny fall afternoon?

Cassian walked down the hallway toward us with the saddest look I'd ever seen. He stopped in front of me, and Alexandria stood to hug her oldest son. "Cassian, I'm so glad you got here. Do you know anything about what happened?"

Frowning, he shook his head. "No, Mom. He told me he had some errands to run after we talked first thing this morning. I think he mentioned going to see someone at the produce company we use because we've been having problems with the deliveries for the past few weeks. Do they know where this happened?"

I looked up at him and answered for her. "The police told me when I got here that it happened in Dade City and that they had some guy in custody. They said something about a witness too, but I don't think I was paying close enough attention."

Cassian leaned down and kissed me softly on the top of the head. "Let me go find someone and see what's going on. We need to find out what happened. What about Kane? Is he in surgery?"

Nodding, I pulled Liam closer as I answered, "He's still in surgery. They said they'd come find me when he got out."

"Well, then let me find out what's going on with the police."

I reached out and squeezed his hand as my tears

threatened to overwhelm me again. "Thank you."

"I'll be back. Stay positive. He's tough, Abbi. Kane's going to be fine."

As Cassian walked away and Alexandria repeated what he said, I prayed to God they were right. I didn't know what I'd do if they weren't.

CASSIAN RETURNED WITH THE NEWS that Kane had been shot with a .38 at close range by a man named Rick Branton. The police didn't have any more details, but they suspected it might be a drug deal gone bad.

"That's crazy, Cassian," I said. Alexandria took the baby from my arms, and I began to pace back and forth across the tile floor in the waiting room. "Kane wouldn't be involved with anything like that. No way."

He shook his head angrily. "I told them that. They don't know what happened, but they told me it happened on Chestnut Street in Dade City."

I stopped dead and spun around to face him. "Chestnut Street? Where?"

"I don't know. Why? Does he know someone there?"

Stefan joined us and hugged me to him before answering his brother's question. "Sebastian Thorne lives on Chestnut Street in Dade City. That's where we were the other night. Did he have something to do with this?"

Cassian seemed confused. "I don't understand.

What would Kane be doing at Sebastian's house in the middle of the day and why would someone there with him have a gun?"

Nobody said anything to answer his questions, so finally I said, "He wanted to tell him the truth. I know that. I know he wanted Sebastian to know he had brothers in you guys."

A sheepish look came over Stefan's face, and Cassian snapped at him. "Do you see what's happened because of all of this digging up the past? You couldn't just leave well enough alone? Why couldn't you and Kane just leave it be?"

Quickly, Alexandria jumped in and stopped him. "Your brothers had good intentions, Cassian. I know why Kane would want to let Sebastian know about you three."

"He didn't want him to not know where he came from," I said quietly. "I think he saw a lot of himself in Sebastian."

"Well, I don't," Cassian said angrily. "All I see is trouble and that's all I've ever seen from the minute Kane and Stefan brought it up. But if Sebastian was there, I want to know if he was shot too."

He stormed away, and Stefan took me in his arms again to hug me tightly to him. "I'm so sorry, Abbi. I never dreamed anything like this would happen. I just wanted to find out about this guy. That's all."

I let myself cry again and said through the tears, "I

don't blame you, Stefan. Kane was going to find out about him whether you or Cassian wanted to. He'd already made up his mind."

"I swear we didn't think anything like this would happen, Abbi." Stefan pulled away and looked into my eyes. "Kane would never put himself in danger of being taken away from you and the kids, even for a brother."

"Yes, he would," I said with a smile, knowing what family meant to Kane. "He just wouldn't think he'd get hurt."

I returned to pacing until I saw Cash walking towards us a few minutes later with a look of rage on his face. Unsure I wanted to know the cause, fearing he'd found out that something had happened to Kane, I still needed to ask what was wrong.

"Did something happen? Did you hear something about Kane?"

My heart sank in the millisecond between my asking and his answering. My head began to swim as the horrifying thought of Kane gone from the world sunk in. My legs began to give out as I collapsed into one of the waiting room chairs.

Cash rushed to my side and quickly explained, "No, I heard nothing. That's not what I went to find out about."

I listened to his words and slowly realized he hadn't just told me the worst news I could ever hear. "I saw your face and you looked so furious. I just thought…"

My words trailed off as I began to sob, and Cash hugged me to him. "No, it's okay. I think he's still in surgery. Don't give up on him, Abbi. He's strong. He'll make it through this."

I tried to believe him, to believe that everything would be okay, but a tiny, terrible thought weaved its way through my mind. What if this was it? What if after everything he'd been through this was the one thing he couldn't overcome?

Cash's body tensed against mine, so I looked up to see why and there stood Sebastian just a few feet away. He looked so much like Kane.

I wiped my eyes and sat up straight in my seat. "How did this happen, Sebastian?"

That's all I wanted to know. How did the man I love end up getting shot while he was at his house?

He hung his head and said softly, "I'm so sorry. I never thought Rick would do anything like that. It all happened so fast. I couldn't stop it."

"Rick? You know the person who shot Kane? This wasn't a robbery?"

Sebastian lifted his head and nodded.

I couldn't believe this. One of Sebastian's friends had shot Kane? "I want you to tell me why your friend Rick shot my husband," I said so loudly that everyone in the waiting area turned and looked at me.

My voice frightened Liam and he started crying, so Alexandria hurried out of the room with him. I waited for Sebastian's answer, but he said nothing and simply looked down at his hands folded in front of him.

I stood up and screamed, "Tell me! Tell me why this happened!"

Cash and Stefan moved to stand on either side of me, and Sebastian shook his head. "I got myself into something I shouldn't have and Rick came looking for money I owed him. I didn't have it, so Kane was reaching into his pocket to give him the money he had. Rick must have thought he was reaching for a gun and that's when he shot him."

Stunned by what he said, I stared at his face, suddenly hating everything about him. I wanted to pound my fists against his chest to make him feel as bad as I felt. I wanted him to know how much this hurt.

Cash took a step toward him and snapped, "Got yourself into something you shouldn't have? Let me guess. Drugs. Some fucking drug deal went bad and now Kane is fighting for his life."

"No, it wasn't anything like that. Rick and I had been doing some break-in jobs, but Kane was trying to talk me out of doing any more. That's what he was doing at my place today. Trying to convince me to stop."

"Like that makes it any better?" I screamed. "You've been nothing but trouble from the minute Kane started with all this. He worried you'd be dangerous to us so he lied to me about you. He continued to try to find out about you even though one of his brothers wanted no part of it. And what did he get for all of it?"

Sebastian began to say he was sorry again, but I didn't want to hear it anymore. "Don't! Your apologies won't change the fact that Kane got shot when it should have been you. Go away! I don't want to see you ever again!"

My outburst shocked him. Horrified by what I'd said, he opened his mouth to speak but nothing came out. Finally, he turned around and walked away.

I didn't care that I'd hurt his feelings. He'd gotten the man I love hurt.

Chapter Eleven

Sebastian

Racing toward the door to get the hell out of that damned hospital, I tried to put everything Kane's wife had said out of my mind. I wasn't to blame for Kane getting shot. I never asked him to show up at my place to lecture me on my fucking life. He had some kind of hard on for being my brother, but I didn't need him or those other two in my life.

Not that I was happy about him getting hurt because of me. I wasn't. He'd been a pretty decent guy, overall. Well, after that night he and Stefan found me drunk and brought me home. That night he'd been sort of a hard ass dick, but even that didn't make me happy that he was lying on that operating table with his chest cut open fighting to live.

If only Rick hadn't found out about the other night.

I stopped just outside the doors to catch my breath and inhaled some asshole's most recent drag of cigarette. Turning to see a guy with a long, greasy ponytail standing way too fucking close to the building, I barked, "Can't you fucking read? There are sick people here. Like they need that shit in their lungs. If you want to kill yourself slowly, do it fifty feet away where you're supposed to be."

He shot back with some bullshit response about it being a free country as he began to walk toward the parking lot, but I didn't hear most of it. I didn't ask for his opinion on how much the world didn't want to deal with his secondhand smoke.

I took another deep breath to clear my head, and at least this one wasn't full of nicotine and shit that would give me lung cancer. Finding a bench away from the door, I sat down and closed my eyes, trying to push this whole day out of my mind.

Someone sat down next to me and said, "Abbi's just really scared."

I looked over and saw Stefan. "I know. I didn't mean for any of this to happen."

He nodded and gave me a weak smile. "Kane's tough. He'll pull through."

A twinge of regret pinched at me. I barely knew either of them, but this guy was sitting here with me trying to make me feel better, even though I probably didn't deserve it.

"Why don't you think I'm public enemy number one like they do in there?"

Stefan blew the air out of his lungs and shrugged. "I

know how much letting you know we existed meant to Kane. Means to Kane."

I turned toward him, needing some answers about this whole brother thing Kane had going on. "Why is that exactly?"

A big smile spread across his face. "You have to understand Kane isn't like me or Cash."

"I know. He told me he had a different mother."

"I guess you'd call her different. She pretty much tortured him his entire life because he had our father for a dad. She wasn't exactly mother of the year. Kane's mother wanted him to be with them, but well, our father wasn't exactly father of the year either. So Kane got the worst of both worlds.

"Fuck." The guy had gotten both barrels of crap growing up.

"Yeah. It was pretty bad, from what he's told me. She took out her anger on him. She never let him forget his father didn't want them. I mean, she named him Kane, for fuck's sake. You know, like Cain and Abel. He had the misfortune of looking like our dad, so that didn't make things any better for him growing up either."

Just hearing about Kane's childhood made me depressed. I'd never known anything about my father, but that was better than hearing shit about him every day of my life.

"So that's why he was so jacked up about finding

out about me?"

"Yeah. I think he sees himself in you."

Since Stefan seemed to be in a confessing kind of mood, I asked, "So how did you three get so close if he's from a different mother?"

"My father, I mean our father, made it a requirement in his will that if we wanted to inherit anything we needed to work together at a business and make it successful. So the three of us started a club, and once it became a success, we got our inheritances."

Now I was even more curious about this father I never knew about. "Inheritance?"

Stefan nodded, running his hands through his hair. "You know, I think that's another reason Kane was so into finding you. I'm sorry our father never did anything for you. As I said, he wasn't father of the year. In fact, I'd venture a guess that only my brother Cash has anything really great to say about him."

"Cash? I'm guessing he's the one who definitely doesn't like me," I said, remembering how angry the other guy was inside.

"Yeah, that's Cash. He's the oldest of the three of us. Cash got my father's name and all his attention growing up. He was the heir, and I was the spare."

"And Kane and I were the bastards he didn't give a fuck about."

For a moment, it looked like what I said pissed Stefan off, but finally he nodded in agreement. "I guess that's an accurate description of it all. Cash was the apple of my father's eye. He looked like him, had his name, and my father always let him know how much he thought of him. Cash was the golden child. I was too much like my mother. She's the woman inside with Abbi."

Now I was really confused. "Wait a second. Your mother is in there with Abbi worrying about the son that her husband had with some woman?"

Chuckling, he patted me on the shoulder. "Welcome to the family. It must look pretty fucked up from an outsider's point of view, I guess, but yeah, she loves Kane as much as she loves Cash and me."

I tried to imagine how that worked but couldn't. "No offense, but yeah, that seems fucked up."

"That's my mother for you. She loved my father so she accepted how he was. Now she accepts the people who came from that."

We sat there outside the hospital entrance for a few minutes saying nothing until I had to ask why he wanted to get to know me. "So I know why Kane was curious about me, but why were you?"

Stefan looked off in the distance and thought about my question for a while before turning to look at me. "To be honest, I wasn't sure. I knew Kane was all about it and Cash wanted nothing to do with finding you, but I wasn't sure one way or another. It was my girlfriend who convinced me to at least find out. I figured I had nothing to lose."

"You don't mind not being the youngest anymore?"

"I'm my mother's youngest and always have been, so that's not a problem. I figured my father had other kids out there after me anyway. And it's not like I ever got anything from being his second kid, to be honest. I was the spare."

Something in the way Stefan kept saying that made me feel like he'd had some of that same shittiness Kane had lived through growing up. This Cassian March guy had created a lot of grief for people in his life, it seemed.

"I have to tell you it's freaking me out a little knowing that I look so much like these two other people. I joked, halfway serious, with Kane when he came over today that he was me from the future. You know, like you see on TV. I think your brother could be me from the future but really pissed off."

Laughing, Stefan nodded. "Cash isn't so bad. He's just a different kind of person from you and me. He and Kane are serious people. We're not. Our father was serious like them."

"I'm guessing it's nice to look like your own person like you do, though," I said as I studied how different Stefan looked from the three of us.

He stood from the bench and looked down at me. "Yes and no. It pretty much just makes me odd man out. I better get back in there, but I wanted to make sure you knew this whole finding you thing meant a lot to Kane." Stefan frowned and said, "Means a lot to him."

"I hope you're right about him being tough enough to handle this. I never meant for anything like this to happen. I wish Kane had listened to me when I told him to slip out the window when Rick got there."

"That's not like him. Kane's thing is saving people. Always has been. It might be the only good thing that came from growing up with that mother of his."

Stefan left me sitting there wishing I'd gotten to know Kane better before all this happened. I still didn't know if I wanted anything to do with having three brothers all of a sudden, but from what I'd learned about Kane, I liked him.

I'd never had a big brother. I didn't need saving, but it might have been cool to know someone had my back. But even if he survived, I doubted he'd want anything to do with me now. Not when his wife and one of his brothers blamed me for what happened.

It was nice while it lasted, though.

Chapter Twelve

ABBI

THE DOCTOR CAME OUT AFTER what seemed like forever and let us know Kane had come through surgery okay but the following days would tell how he would do long term. The bullet did a lot of damage, even nicking his heart, but the doctor believed they'd found all of it, so now we just had to pray his body could do what it had to so he could be up and around again.

I smiled as he spoke the words, hearing them without really hearing what he was saying. All I could think of was Kane lying in that bed as he fought to stay with the ones he loved. I knew he would fight, but would he be strong enough now to overcome what that bullet did?

When they finally took me to see him, the shock of him lying in that hospital bed with all those tubes and wires attached to him almost made me burst into tears. I'd watched him sleeping many times as he lay next to me in bed, still except for his chest rising and falling with each breath. Even asleep, Kane always looked strong and powerful.

But now, his power looked like it had been sapped from him, leaving the outside of Kane intact but not the inside.

I sat down at his bedside and took his hand in mine. I loved the feel of his long fingers intertwined with my much smaller ones. Their harshness touching my softness always struck me as something memorable.

The nurses left me alone with him, so I did what I always did when I was worried about us. I talked. I didn't know if he understood what I was saying or even heard me, but if there was the slightest chance he did, I needed him to know I was there with him.

"Kane, I'm right here. You're not alone, and I promise I won't leave here until you open your eyes and tell me you're going to fine. Liam and Annalea are with Alexandria, so you don't have to worry. After you and me, there's no one we can trust more with our babies than their grandmother."

I stopped for a moment, the emotion of the moment choking me. The last time the kids had been out at Alexandria's, Kane and I had enjoyed a rare night of romance. Now days later, they were back at her house, and we were here in a hospital as he recovered from being shot.

How quickly things could change.

Taking a deep breath, I pushed aside my sadness

and continued to talk to him about all the things he'd miss if he didn't survive this.

"You know, when I was out in the waiting room with Liam, I was looking at him as he played with my hair and realized for the first time that he's so much like you with that. You've always loved playing with my hair. Do you remember that first night at your apartment on top of Club X? My hair was much shorter then, but as I lay in your arms and drifted off to sleep, feeling safer than I'd felt in so long, you played with the ends of my hair. I don't think I've ever told you how much I loved that."

Tears welled in my eyes at the memory of that night. So sullen and dark, still he saved me from yet another mistake I'd made in my life. He took me to that shabby apartment of his, and there in those rooms that reminded me of a cell the first time I saw them, he wrapped his arms around me and protected me from the world.

I'd been in love with him since that very night. He was everything to me. My husband. The father of my children. The man I adored more than even mere words could express.

We'd been through hell and back since that night, and through it all, I believed no matter what the rest of the world saw in this man, they were wrong. He wasn't cold or cruel or even angry. He should have been after all he'd had to endure growing up, but he wasn't.

Beneath that gruff exterior beat the heart of a man who could love harder and more intensely than anyone I'd ever met.

And now that heart had been invaded by a bullet over some stupid fool's mistakes.

Anger bubbled up inside me. I hated Sebastian for Kane getting hurt. I didn't know if it was right, but it didn't matter as I sat there watching a respirator move my husband's chest up and down.

I couldn't focus on that now, though. I needed to stay positive for him, so I kissed his rough knuckles and forced away my feelings about his brother in favor of remembering the times Kane and I had shared.

"Do you remember that night when Annalea was three when we all drove up to that place in Georgia because you couldn't believe I'd never had real Georgia peaches? You made Annalea promise not to tell me where we were going. We piled into the Mustang, and I thought we were going to the beach since you'd mentioned it earlier that day. Annalea giggled practically the whole way there as I kept asking where we were going and you kept telling me to trust you. I swear, I thought she was going to explode by the time we reached the farm."

I looked up at his face and saw his dark eyelashes still resting on his cheeks. His stony expression hadn't changed, but I had to continue. I couldn't let him think he was alone there in that cold hospital room.

"Those were the best peaches I've ever had in my life. But what was even better was the smile on your face as you watched me eat my first one. The juices rolled down my chin onto my shirt, and I tried to mop it all up with a napkin, and there you were smiling at me as I made a mess of myself on my first real Georgia peach. Do you remember that, Kane? I'll never forget how happy my eating that peach made you."

I wanted to see that smile again. I wanted to see those beautiful blue eyes of his light up when he looked at me. I wanted to hear him tell me how much he loved me as he held me in his arms.

As the sadness began to overwhelm me, I let myself cry as I sat there holding his hand and wishing for him to come back to me. "You have to get through this, Kane. We have so much to look forward to. Our whole lives are in front of us, baby. I can't do this without you. Who's going to intimidate Annalea's boyfriends when she starts dating? Who's going to teach Liam how to play football and baseball or whatever sport he wants to play when he gets older?"

My tears dropped onto his forearm as I thought about all the important times he'd miss if he left us now. It wasn't just that I needed him for our kids, though. I needed him for me. From that moment he held me in his arms as we lay on the floor of his apartment, I knew I didn't want to be without him ever again. We'd spent months apart when I was pregnant with Annalea, but since then, he'd been by my side protecting me and loving me as the most important part of my life.

I didn't know what I'd do if I lost that.

"Kane, I need you to know I can't imagine life without you. Life without that crooked smile you give me when you're not really listening to what I'm saying but don't want me to know. I know, but I like that smile anyway. Or life without hearing you say my name when you crawl into bed at night. That deep way you say it like it's the one word you've been waiting all day to speak and then pull me close to be next to you as we sleep. Please don't make me live without those things. Please don't make me live without you. Don't leave me, Kane."

I should have been used to him silently listening to me as I spoke. I'd always been the talker in the relationship. Kane was more interested in showing how he felt instead of telling anyone. At that moment, I would have given anything for him to say just one simple word.

Closing my eyes, I let my mind wander back to all those days and nights that made up our life. Unlike in books and movies, the time two people spend together isn't all fireworks and incredible moments. Most of our time together consisted of the regular events of life— the comings and goings that happened every workday, the rote answers we gave to the same old questions to let each other know that amidst the commonplace events of our lives we loved one another.

The small smile he put on when he wanted to show me he was listening to whatever I was saying but really wanted to close his eyes and fall asleep with me in his arms.

My way of gently stroking the top of his hand when he was angry about something that told him I knew his rage wasn't directed at me but at the rest of the world.

How when work at the restaurant got to be too much he'd come home to me to rest his head on my shoulder as we lay in bed and listen to my stories of how Annalea and Liam did something so incredibly cute that day.

We had changed from the people we were when we first met all those years ago at Club X, and to some we surely would be seen as boring, but it was those small gestures from both of us that made our life together so dear to me.

As I thought about everything we shared, my favorite memory of our time together surfaced in my mind. When I became pregnant with Liam, Kane had promised that pregnancy would be different than my first. I knew he felt guilty about the time apart with Annalea, but he didn't have to be.

I understood the demons he fought every day then. I knew them well and hated them, but I didn't blame him.

So every day he made sure I knew how happy he was that I was carrying his child again. I'd never felt so loved in my life.

And when the day came for Liam to finally arrive, it was Kane who was by my side when that precious soul made his entrance into the world. Exhausted but happy, I watched as he took our son into his arms and his eyes filled with tears as he first looked at him.

"You have a son, Mr. Jackson. Meet your little boy," the nurse said as she handed him to his father.

Never one for saying much, he simply stared at the tiny human in his hold and smiled. Curious to know what he thought, I asked, "Does he look like me or you?"

Kane tilted Liam toward me and beamed his happiness. With his dark hair and blue eyes, he looked just like his father. "I think this one got my genes," he joked.

"We never decided on a boy's name," I said as he came around the bed to show me my son. "What are we going to call him?"

He didn't take his eyes off him but shook his head. "I have no idea. All I know is he's beautiful, Abbi."

I looked at the incredible human being we'd made from love and leaned my cheek against Kane's arm. "Liam. Liam Alexander Jackson."

"Liam, this is your mom. She's the person who showed me I deserved love and all the great things that come with it. She's one of a kind and you're lucky to have her as your mother. Never forget that."

I looked up at Kane and smiled as he handed the baby to me. "I love you. You know that?"

He leaned over and kissed me softly on the lips and then kissed Liam on the forehead. "I do, and I love you, angel."

"I hope he grows up to be just like his father," I said as I looked down at our son.

"And I hope he has a lot of his mother in him."

I lifted my head to look up at Kane now as he lay in that hospital bed and saw that man who saved me when I desperately needed it. He was scarred and broken still from all those years growing up, but the parts of him I loved the most came from the pain he'd suffered. It had made him someone whose love was gentle and steadfast, exactly the kind of love he'd never felt when he was a child.

If only I could save him now, but as usual, he was the one who had to be strong. I prayed to God he could be.

Chapter Thirteen

Cassian

THE DRIVE HOME FROM THE hospital flew by in a blur as I went back and forth between hoping Kane would be okay and hating this new brother of mine for wreaking havoc on my family. Fucking kid! I knew nothing good would come from searching out another of my father's bastards.

By the time I reached the condo, my stomach had twisted itself into knots over this whole damn thing. I needed to calm down or Olivia and the baby would be the ones who paid for that asshole kid's mistake. I was too emotional, but I couldn't help it.

Kane was more than just my brother. He was one of the few people in the world I truly cared about.

Olivia sat waiting for me, and as soon as I got through the door, I saw the look of concern in her eyes. "How is he, Cash? I tried calling Stefan and your mother when you didn't answer your phone, but all I got were their voicemails."

I poured myself a stiff drink and downed it quickly

before pouring another glass of scotch. "Sorry. I turned it onto silent at the hospital and must have forgotten to change it back when I left."

She walked up to me and wrapped her arms around me in an embrace I needed so badly. "Oh, honey. He's going to be okay. I just know it. Kane's got everything in the world to live for. He'll pull through."

Hanging my head, I let it drop onto her shoulder as I silently prayed she was right. "He made it through surgery, but now we'll have to see how he does in the next few days. The bullet hit his heart, so the doctor's concerned that there might be irreparable damage."

I heard her gasp at the news. Pulling me to her, she said quietly, "I'm so sorry, honey."

I didn't want to hear anyone's apologies. I wanted my brother to be okay. I wanted him to be out of that hospital bed and back at the restaurant with me like he should have been that day. And I was fucking pissed he couldn't do any of that and might never be able to again.

Backing away from her, I shook my head. "This should have never happened. If only he hadn't gone searching for that goddamned brother of ours. I knew it was a fucking mistake."

"It was important to Kane that he got to know him, Cash. You weren't going to change his mind from that. You know him."

Suddenly, I couldn't stop my anger from exploding

out of me. I didn't want to hear any more talk about how much Kane wanted to find out about Sebastian. I should have done more to stop him.

"Don't use the past tense, Olivia! He's not dead!"

My words echoed off the walls of the condo, surprising her. Hurt by my outburst, she frowned and said, "I didn't mean to act like there was no hope, Cash. I'm sorry."

Christ, I was lashing out at the one person who loved me no matter what. She began to cry, so I took her in my arms and let her sob against me like I should. I was her husband. It was my duty to be there for her when everything in the world seemed to be going wrong.

"I'm sorry, Olivia. I didn't mean to yell like that. You didn't do anything wrong, baby."

"I'm afraid too, Cash," she said through her tears. "I love your brothers like they're my own. My heart is broken over this."

I cradled her face, pressing my forehead to hers. "I know, and I shouldn't have snapped like that. I'm just so angry about this whole Sebastian thing."

Olivia looked into my eyes in that way that never failed to calm me. "He's going to be okay."

Taking a deep breath, I let it out, wishing it would take all my fears with it. But that didn't happen. "What if Kane can't pull through? He's come so far from where he was when our father forced us to work together. For him to lose everything over this…"

My emotions began to spin out of control. They swung from anger to sadness and then out of the blue I began to laugh, as if anything about this whole thing was funny at all.

The look on Olivia's face showed how horrified she was by my behavior. "What are you laughing about?"

"My father. Wherever he is, he's just where he's always been when trouble happens. Nowhere to be found. He fathers all of us without a thought, and then he goes and dies. On top of that, then we get to find out that he wants to be our father from the afterlife and make the three of us work together. Pure Cassian March bullshit."

"Cash, are you okay?" Olivia asked as I downed the rest of my second scotch.

I had just gotten started.

"Stefan and I could barely stand each other when he died, and he thought throwing another person into the mix was a good idea. I remember the first time I saw Kane. It was like his face screamed, 'I'm a March.' But he wasn't. He looked like my father, just like I did, but I was a March. He was the child my father had from cheating on my mother."

I stopped as my mind whirled with memories of how many times I heard my mother cry herself to sleep waiting for my father to return at night, knowing he was out with some woman. And then to add to the indignity, he couldn't even be bothered to make sure he didn't father any more fucking kids.

"And I didn't even have it the worst. Stefan had spent his life trying to make my father happy, to make him see that he had another son other than me. He never did. And then in death, he made sure Stefan understood how much he didn't fucking care by giving Kane part of his money. I've never told Stefan this, Olivia, but I understood why he was so angry for so long. Part of it was my fault, but then Kane came along and it was like having two versions of our father forever lording over him. No wonder he hated the two of us all those years."

Gently stroking my arm, Olivia quietly said, "You're upset. I know. It's going to be okay."

I shook my head. "No, but we've never been okay. Thanks to my father, we've always been fucked up. Cash, the perfect son because he didn't dare be anything else. Stefan, the perpetual lost boy because his father never gave a damn about him. And Kane, the child he didn't even bother to own up to until it was too late."

My chest hurt from everything I was feeling. The anger. The rage. The sadness and fear. All of it pressed down on me like a weight I feared would never leave.

"Honey, maybe we should get you something to eat since you're probably starving and I think those two drinks are having an effect on you?"

I waved her off, needing to say what was on my mind, even if she didn't understand what I meant and even if I sounded like a fucking madman.

"Now after all that we've been through, my father has his hand in more pain for us. Another son. Like we need another brother. Of course, Kane wanted to find out about him. For all that tough façade he has, inside he's still that kid whose mother emotionally beat him up every day of his life because of who his father was. He's still that bastard Cassian March didn't claim. I should have known that one day he'd want to find Sebastian."

"You couldn't have stopped him, Cash."

I turned to face her and winced. "I should have, though. Do you know how long I've known about the other ones? It feels like all my life I've known Stefan and I weren't the only kids he had. For me, it was easy not to think of them. I didn't want to go through everything we went through when Kane came into our lives."

"But that turned out good for all three of you. Maybe this thing with Sebastian could turn out good too."

"Yeah, because it's gone swimmingly so far. He's a fall down drunk and a thief who got Kane shot because he owed some guy money he cheated him out of. Hell, he may be more like my father than any of us, Olivia."

She pulled me to her and hugged me, probably

worried I was going to spin out of control at any minute. Maybe I would. I didn't know how to handle what was happening with Kane. I'd gone from resenting him, to tolerating him, to liking the son of a bitch at times, to honestly loving him like a brother. I didn't know how to deal with the real possibility that tomorrow he might not be here anymore.

And that it would be just Stefan and me again because there was no way in hell I was ever going to accept Sebastian as my brother. I didn't care that he looked like my father or had his DNA swirling inside him.

"It's going to be okay, Cash," she said as she softly ran her hands over my back. "He's going to be okay."

But what if he wasn't?

"I don't know what to do, Olivia. I'm angry, sad, and scared to death all at the same time. I wasn't even like this when Kane got arrested."

She leaned away from me and smiled, gently stroking the side of my face. "Well, then you knew what to do. You got the lawyer to do his job, threw money at the problem, and waited for it to be solved."

"That's me, huh? Shallow prick who solves problems by tossing money at them?" I asked as I hung my head.

"No, that's not who you are, but then you had a way of fixing the problem. That's who you are, Cash. You handle things, but now you can't. Now you have to leave it up to Kane to fix this. You don't think he will?"

I closed my eyes and thought about Abbi and those two beautiful kids of his. "If there's a way for him to get past this and be with Abbi, Annalea, and Liam, I think he's going to fight like he's never fought for anything before in his life. I'm just worried there is no way, that the second that bullet entered his body, he had all his choices taken away from him, and for what?"

It always came back to that question. Kane had possibly given up everything for some guy who he shared a father with. A father who never fucking cared enough to be there for either one of them.

Olivia softly kissed my lips and whispered, "For family. It's why all three of you brothers do nearly everything."

"Ironic, isn't it? We come from the world's worst father, yet we all value family enough to risk everything for it."

"Your father may have been the world's worst, but your mother is pretty damn terrific. You get your love of family from her, Cash, not from your father. Alexandria deserves all the credit."

I nodded and thought about how much my mother had been through because of my father, and yet still she considered Kane her son like Stefan and me. And I knew if Kane became close to Sebastian, she'd accept him eventually too. She'd probably even push for me to come around about him.

No matter how I felt about Sebastian, I hoped Kane had the chance to try to convince me too.

My cell rang, and I saw it was my mother calling. Answering, I heard panic in her voice. "Cassian, you need to get back to the hospital."

"Why? Did something happen?" Fear tore through me at the thought that Kane had taken a turn for the worse.

"They had to take Kane back into surgery. He went into cardiac arrest. Abbi needs you and Stefan. Tell Olivia I'll watch the baby so she and Shay can get there too."

I ended the call, feeling like the world had begun spinning out of control. Olivia hurried to get Cassian ready to go to my mother's as I prayed to God I got to my brother in time.

Chapter Fourteen

Kane

THE TOUCH OF ABBI'S HAND on mine told me I was still okay. At least I wanted to believe I was, but the sound of beeping machines and people yelling made me think things were anything but okay.

As long as I felt Abbi's hand holding mine, I didn't worry.

I tried to remember what happened, but my thoughts were hazy, like my brain was disconnected. I was at Sebastian's trying to convince him to give up stealing for a living. Some guy busted in demanding money from him. I wanted to give him what I had to at least give Sebastian some time.

After that, everything went dark. I remembered a popping sound and a smell I hadn't experienced in years. Then nothing, other than the feel of Abbi's hand touching mine as she talked about Annalea and Liam. I wanted to open my eyes and tell her I loved her, but I couldn't do either.

I knew by the sound of her voice that something

was wrong. I always knew when she was unhappy, even if I couldn't see her face. I hated hearing her sound like that because it was always from something I'd done. No one else in the world made her sad like I did.

It wasn't something I ever wanted to do. I never set out to hurt her, but I was so fucked up even now that sometimes I made the wrong decisions or said the wrong thing. Or I lied to her, although I knew she hated when I did that. But I lied to protect her, never to make her sad.

Suddenly, I felt her hand drift away, leaving me cold and alone. I wanted to scream, "Don't go! Stay. No matter what I did, I'll fix it, Abbi. I promise I will!"

But I couldn't cry out. I couldn't move. All the yelling and beeping grew louder and louder. Who were these people and what were they saying? Everything sounded frantic and garbled.

Was I dreaming? Was that why I couldn't speak or see?

My heart raced as I tried to wake up, pounding harder than it ever had before. I felt like my chest might explode. I had to calm down or I'd have a damn heart attack. Was I dreaming all of this? What was that thing I heard once about dying in a dream meant you died in real life? Or was it falling?

Fuck! And then there was nothing. No sound. No beeping or screaming. Nothing.

I opened my eyes, and before me I saw a beautiful

sunny day. I stood in the dirt near second base on a baseball field, just off the perfectly green grass. No one else was there with me. No players, no spectators. Nobody.

Just me.

Where was I? I looked around and wondered if I was still dreaming.

"This isn't a dream. Well, not technically," a deep voice said, answering my unspoken question.

I spun around to see him standing there like we belonged together on a baseball diamond. Since I'd never even seen a game with him, much less played baseball together, I had to wonder why I was there with him at all.

"Because this is what you wanted when you were seven. To play baseball and have your father there to see you."

The memory of me begging my mother to let me play on the local team flashed through my mind as vividly as if it had happened just seconds before. I wanted to play more than anything, but she said no. I never told her I wanted my father to see me play. I knew better.

A feeling of sadness filled me at the memory. "I never did get to play."

My father nodded, a frown etched into his features. "I wouldn't have come to see you anyway, if that means anything."

I looked around as my chest began to ache. "If this is a dream, it sucks. Nothing like being told the one person you desperately wanted to love you wouldn't have given a damn."

"This isn't a dream, Kane."

"Okay, Cassian. What is it then?" I asked as I headed toward the outfield to lie down in that green grass that looked so inviting.

He followed me, but probably not for the same reason. "It's sort of a dream but more of a vision."

Looking back at him, I grimaced at the thought that my father had chosen now to visit me. "So now I'm now having visions? Why?"

"Because you can."

I sat down on that perfect green grass, loving the feel of its coolness against my palms, and looked up at him. "And why's that?"

"Because you're dead."

He said those words like they weren't supposed to scare the hell out of me. "What? No! I'm not dead. Why would you say that?"

"Well, not exactly. We don't have a lot of time, so listen to me. I want to tell you something. I've wanted to tell you for a long time, and since you're here now, let me say this."

I jumped to my feet, looking for a way out of this fucking nightmare. "Say whatever you want, but I'm going home."

My father touched my arm, stopping me cold. "Then let me say this before you go wherever you're off to."

I didn't like the way this was sounding. Why wasn't I going home?

"Okay." Maybe listening to what he had to say was how I could get out of there.

He took a deep breath and shook his head like he didn't want to say what was on his mind. "Of all my kids, you got the worst of it, Kane. I know a big part of that was my fault, but you got a double negative in your parents. All the others had mothers who made up for what I lacked. You had the bad luck to have one who didn't."

I choked back emotion, not even sure why what he was saying bothered me. It wasn't like any of this was news to me.

"What I tried to do when you had to go to jail was to make up for all that I'd done wrong, but I know it wasn't enough. I've had a lot of time to figure that out."

"Here in heaven?"

As soon as the words left my mouth, the baseball field and beautiful day full of blue skies disappeared and suddenly we were standing in a white room. I spun around to figure out what had happened, but my father stood as still as a statue, unfazed by the change.

"Not exactly heaven."

"Stop saying not exactly, damnit! What's happening?"

He screwed his face into an expression like he'd just eaten something terrible. "You're in cardiac arrest. Whether you die now or not isn't in your hands anymore, so I better finish what I was saying."

I felt my chest tighten. "Cardiac arrest? How?"

My father took hold of my arm and instantly calmed me. "Listen to what I have to say. You've gotten past what your mother and I did to you. You've got a beautiful wife you love and two wonderful kids. I know why you wanted to find Sebastian, but don't jeopardize your happiness to make up for my failures. He didn't have the childhood you did. He'll be okay. Don't make a mistake you won't be able to come back from, even if it's for the right reasons."

"I didn't want him to go through life not knowing he had brothers," I explained. "I just thought he should know."

Cassian shook his head. "He's not like you, Kane. I knew when he was born that he'd be okay. He had a mother and father who loved him. He never went without because I wasn't around, like you did."

A light began to flood the room, and slowly I began to lose sight of him. "What's happening now?" I asked. "Am I dying?"

I didn't want to die. I wanted to go back to my life with Abbi and our children. To working with Cash at the restaurant. To everything I hadn't accomplished yet.

As he faded away, he said, "I don't know. I just know our time is up now. Remember what I said, Kane. I'm sorry for never being there for you. I'm sorry you didn't get to play baseball or see the mountains or hear me say I was proud of you. I am, though."

I didn't know how he knew that I had wished for all those things when I was a growing up. I didn't know what was happening or how I had gotten to speak to my father again.

All I knew was I wanted to return to Abbi and feel the touch of her hand on mine. I wanted to see my kids again and hold them in my arms.

I wanted to live.

Chapter Fifteen

Kane

Slowly, I opened my eyes to see Abbi staring at me and smiling, her beautiful blue eyes wide with concern. She did that a lot these days since I came home from the hospital. For the first couple months, I don't think she slept a night all the way through. I'd wake up and see her watching me, afraid that I might stop breathing at some point as I slept.

It wasn't until right around Christmas that she trusted I'd be okay if she closed her eyes. I hated that she worried about me. She didn't have to. The doctor had told her that over and over, but it didn't seem to matter.

"Good morning," she said sweetly.

"Good morning. Did you get a full night's sleep?" I asked, hoping to hear she had.

She kissed me softly on the lips and nodded. "I have to take care of the kids. We have a big day ahead of us today. Cash's party begins at noon, so there's no rest for the wicked."

I knew what that answer meant. She hadn't slept much. Again.

As she turned to slip out of bed, I slid my arm around her waist and pulled her back toward me. "Where are you going in such a hurry? I don't hear either of the kids making any noise yet."

She smiled in that way that never failed to make my heart flutter and said, "I figured I'd get a jump on the day."

"I'd rather you get a jump on me," I said with a wink.

Lifting her so she sat on top of me, I ran my hands down her sides until I reached her hips. After months of waiting because of my injury, I was done being a patient. I wanted to be a husband and a man again.

She gently balanced herself on me, awkwardly placing her hands on my chest. Her right palm covered the scar from where the bullet entered my body, but when she realized where her hand was, she quickly pulled it away.

"I really have to get this day started, Kane."

I lifted my hips to let her feel my hard on ready to go. "Feel that? He's ready to get back into the game."

"You say that like it's cute. I've never been worried about that part of you. It's the other parts that concern me."

Squeezing her ass in my hands, I joked, "Do you mean my tongue? Because if you do, don't worry. He's ready to go too, and I haven't forgotten how to make your thighs quiver."

Her expression grew dark. "Stop joking about this, Kane. I don't want to do anything that would make me lose you. You know that."

I cradled her face and pulled her mouth to mine to kiss her long and deep. "You're not going to lose me if we have sex. My heart is fine. The doctor told you that. I had a heart attack because I'd been shot, not because I have a bad heart. I have a great heart, and I'm as healthy as a horse. So climb on and giddy up!"

From down the hallway, I heard Liam cry, "Mommy!" No sex for me this morning.

"Looks like this cowgirl is going to have to take a rain check," Abbi said as she climbed off me.

As she trotted toward the door, I folded my arms behind my head. "I'll be back here tonight, so be ready."

She stopped and looked at me. "You make it sound like something I need to prepare for."

"It's been months since we were together, Abbi. I'm like a man dying of thirst who's getting his first drink in ages. I don't plan on holding back."

A sly smile formed on her beautiful mouth. "Well, then. I guess I better be ready."

EVERYONE HAD GOTTEN TO ALEXANDRIA'S house

before we arrived since getting both kids ready, fed, and into the car had taken far longer than expected, so Abbi and Annalea hurried up the sidewalk to her front door as Liam and I followed behind. As was tradition, Cash's birthday was always celebrated at his mother's, so I expected something big for his thirty-fifth.

"Where are those beautiful babies?" Alexandria asked as she came through the front door with her arms open wide.

Annalea tore up the porch stairs to hug her. "Grandma! We're here for the party."

"We got a chocolate cake for all you chocolate lovers this year," Alexandria announced, much to her granddaughter's delight.

As Annalea ran inside with Abbi, I handed Liam to his grandmother, who eagerly waited to say hello to her youngest grandchild. "The chocolate lovers seem to be happy."

Alexandria squeezed the baby to her and smiled up at me. "I made sure to get a yellow cake for this special little boy since I know he can't have anything chocolate. I think Shay isn't a chocolate lover either, if I'm not mistaken."

"I'll eat the yellow cake too, so you won't have to worry about much in the way of leftovers, Mom."

She studied me for a long moment before saying, "You look good, Kane. It's like the whole thing never happened."

"I'm as healthy as a horse. Now if I could just convince Abbi of that."

We walked into the house and Alexandria quietly said, "She had a very hard time when she thought she might lose you. You can't blame her for being scared."

"I don't blame her, but she has to stop worrying. I've returned to work and returned to everything I used to do before the shooting. I'm not going anywhere anytime soon."

Patting me on the arm, she smiled. "Well, you're just going to have to convince her of that then. I'm sure it will happen eventually. Just give her time."

I wasn't going to tell her that I'd given it more than enough time and planned to put an end to all this worry that night.

While she took Liam into the kitchen to join his sister and mother, I spied Stefan and Shay outside in the yard. Happy to see them, I made my way out to the porch.

"What's up with you two? Avoiding all the kids inside?"

Shay turned around and smiled. "You know us. We don't want to get too close or we might want one of our own."

"How the hell are you?" Stefan asked as I walked down the stairs to meet them on the grass.

"I'm fine. You're not going to ask me how I'm feeling now too, are you?" I joked.

Slapping me on the shoulder, he laughed. "Not really my style, you know? I'm going to assume you feel fine until I hear otherwise."

That's what I liked about Stefan and Cash. They didn't hover, even though I knew they were worried about me when everything happened.

"Thank God."

Shay opened her arms and gave me a hug. "Well, forget that manly nonsense. I want to know how you're doing, Kane. I haven't seen you since you were in the hospital."

She squeezed me like she was afraid I'd run away if she loosened her hold and then stepped back quickly, like she'd remembered how much Abbi didn't like when she showed me any kind of attention, nice or not.

"I'm fine. I was just telling Alexandria that I'm as healthy as a horse. Now if I could just get everyone to believe me."

Studying me for a moment, Shay seemed to doubt that was the truth for a second, but then she nodded. "You look great. I'm so happy you're okay, Kane."

"Always."

Behind me, Cash yelled from the porch, "It's my birthday and you don't even bother to say hi when you get here? No respect for the birthday boy."

I turned to see him smiling and knew he wasn't angry. "You looked pretty busy with the kids, so I figured I'd let you be the man of the hour. Anything to take the focus off me for once."

"Well, I expect you guys to be in here for the cake in a few minutes, and Stefan, Mom wants you in the kitchen to help her."

Stefan chuckled. "Duty calls."

He ran off toward the house, leaving Shay and me alone for one of the first times in years. Shay instantly seemed awkward, but after a few seconds she asked, "Are you going to continue getting to know Sebastian? Stefan told me he's started contacting you guys again."

Sebastian had called once or twice since I got out of the hospital, but I hadn't spoken to him yet because I didn't know what I wanted to say. I didn't blame him for what happened, but I knew Abbi did. More worry about me was the last thing she needed right now.

"I don't know. Is Stefan?"

Shay nodded, but I saw a sadness come over her face. "I think so. He's all about the idea that he has a younger brother out there."

"You don't look happy about that."

She pressed her lips together to stop herself from speaking for a long moment and turned away. Finally, she turned to face me and said, "Do you mind if I give you some unsolicited advice, Kane?"

We hadn't talked like this since that night in my apartment over Club X, so I was intrigued about what she would say. "Feel free. Say what's on your mind."

"Forget Sebastian. Your wife blames him for what

happened to you, so spending any time with him is going to upset her. Do what you did with me. Forget whatever you want to do and never look back because whatever friendship will give you can't trump the happiness you have with Abbi."

Shay and I had never spoken about how I'd abandoned our friendship because it upset Abbi. She knew and never said anything about it, and even though I missed talking to her, I accepted the reality that what I'd done the night of Annalea's birth had set in motion the hatred Abbi felt for her.

"I'm sorry, Shay. If I hadn't been such a bastard to her all those months, none of it would have happened. I think her feelings toward you are more about how she never forgave me for what I did. Not that I think she should."

"She forgave you, Kane."

I hung my head, hating that this whole thing with Shay and Abbi was all my fault. "Well, she shouldn't have. Some things shouldn't be forgiven."

"I forgave you because I love you."

A look of horror settled into Shay's face as we both saw Abbi standing next to us. I'd been so deep in feeling like shit that I hadn't seen her walk up.

"Abbi, I—"

She shook her head. "No, let me say what I have to say." She turned to look at Shay and smiled. "I'm sorry I let this go on so long that my husband doesn't even feel comfortable talking with you. I've been stupid and petty because of my own insecurities, and that's not right. I hope you can forgive me."

Stunned, Shay said nothing as Abbi hugged her. I had no idea what had brought this on, but I loved her for it.

"Abbi, I don't know what to say. I'm happy we can all be friends now."

"Me too. Again, I'm sorry for everything. I hope you understand, but I need to speak to Kane now. We'll be right in for cake."

Shay smiled and headed into the house as I stood stunned by what had just happened. Abbi waited until she was out of earshot and took my hand in hers.

"I think it's about time I apologized to you too. I'm sorry, Kane. I haven't been a very good wife to you." Her blue eyes welled with tears. "I wanted to be…"

"Don't do this, Abbi. You've been a wonderful wife. You've had to deal with all my nightmarish shit and never once walked away, even when you should have. When I was in the hospital, I knew as long as I could feel your hand holding mine that I was okay."

"I would never leave you. Never. I knew who you were when we started this that night in your rooms above the club. I also knew I loved you. So why would I leave?"

I brought her hand to my lips and kissed it, loving the gentle scent of flowers from her skin. "Because I put you through hell all those months after I sent you away. Because I still forget how wonderful my life is now and think I'm that person I was before I met you."

Abbi wrapped her arms around me as I continued. "Because I lied to you and ended up getting myself shot because I couldn't stop tilting at windmills."

"You don't see all the wonderful things about you. You never have. I do, though. I've seen them since you took me out of that club to protect me."

I pulled back away from her and cradled her face. "I'm not going to do anything else with Sebastian. What Shay said is right. I don't want to jeopardize our happiness. Sebastian's fine. He grew up with a mother who loved him. He's not like me."

Abbi's face lit up from her smile. "I know you're worried I hate him. I did. When I was sitting in that hospital room praying to God you'd live, all I could think of was how he was to blame for you lying in that bed. I know that's not true, though. I know how much family means to you, so if you need to be around him, I just need you to promise me you won't lie to me anymore."

"I don't know. Maybe I will find him again, but right now, I have all the family I need."

Standing on her toes, she kissed me sweetly on the lips. "Well, if you decide you want a relationship with him, I'm behind you one hundred percent. I just need to be sure there won't be any more lies between us."

"I promise. No more lies."

"Good. Let's go inside and celebrate your brother's birthday and tonight we'll have our own celebration," she said with a twinkle in her eye.

"What's this change about? Not that I don't like it, because I do, but this morning you were worried I might drop dead from sex."

She pulled me toward the house. "Let's just say I was reminded that I have a very sexy man for a husband and I realized worrying about everything was a waste."

I didn't really care what had changed her mind. I knew she'd tell me eventually. Until then, it was nice to be back to the way we were before I got shot.

Epilogue

Kane

Opening the bedroom door, I saw all the lights were dark. I'd tucked Liam into his crib and told Annalea her favorite nighttime story, but I'd taken too long. Abbi must have drifted off to sleep before I could get to bed.

Disappointed, I stripped out of my clothes and slid under the covers. I didn't blame her. It had been a long day with everyone out at Alexandria's.

I closed my eyes as a sense of happiness came over me that I hadn't felt in a long time. Abbi's problem with Shay was over, and even though I wasn't sure what I wanted to do about Sebastian, I knew whatever I decided, the woman I loved would be by my side.

My time with my father when I was lying in that hospital bed flashed through my mind, and his apology replayed in my head. I'd spent nearly all my life wondering why I wasn't enough for him to love me like a father should. When I became a father to my own children, the question remained.

Now I knew for sure what everyone who loved me had said was true. It wasn't me who was lacking. It was my father.

Abbi slid her hand down my chest and over my stomach to take my cock in her hand. "Hey, are you just going to lie there in the dark or come on over here where your wife has been waiting for you?"

God, I loved this woman.

"I thought you were asleep already. I figured I'd be left to my own devices," I said with a chuckle.

She nuzzled my neck, sending excitement racing through me. "No way, baby. I've been waiting for this celebration all day."

I pulled her on top of me and kissed her deep, my tongue mingling with hers and thrilling me like only she could. "What exactly are we celebrating?" I asked as I lifted my hips to slide into her wet and waiting cunt.

Straddling me, she rolled her hips forward and back as she balanced herself on my chest. "You. Me. Us. Me finally remembering who you are."

I groaned, loving the feel of her wrapped around my cock. It had been too damn long since I was with Abbi like this.

"Did you forget who your husband was?" Holding her hips as she rode me, I added, "Because I never changed."

She stopped moving and sat up straight on me. "I know, but I did. I got scared I'd lose you. Once that settled into my brain, I couldn't see you anymore. You became the man I was terrified would die on me."

We'd never talked about this, but I knew what had happened. I just didn't know how to show her I wasn't going to leave her anytime soon. So for months, she acted like she was afraid every day was the one I'd be snatched away, and I said nothing, too guilty for having put her through all that had happened because of my recklessness.

"I'm glad you can see the real me again, angel."

Abbi leaned forward and kissed me like everything she'd ever needed existed in that kiss. "I want the man I fell in love with back, Kane."

I rolled her over onto her back and slowly began thrusting into her. "Even though he works a lot and doesn't talk as much as you want him to? And even though he might always be fucked up?"

Digging her heels into my back as she urged me to fuck her faster, Abbi pulled me to her and whispered in my ear, "I love that man, no matter how messed up he is. We were broken when we met, and I never wanted anyone but him."

I plunged into her over and over, those studs marking her body just as they had that night we first made love. I'd found something in Abbi that I'd never found in anyone else in the world, and after all we'd gone through, the truth was simple between us.

She was the angel who saved me, no matter how

much she wanted to believe I'd rescued her. She'd accepted me and all the fucked up issues that I brought with me. But whatever else I was—father, son, brother—I was the man who adored her, first and foremost.

There, in that bed we shared as husband and wife, I gave her everything I had and reveled in the amazement that she gave me herself completely and without question.

As she rested her head on my chest where that bullet nearly took me away from her and everyone I loved, I leaned forward and kissed her hair. "Thank you for what you did today. It means the world to me."

Abbi looked up at me and narrowed her eyes. "Why?"

I knew she thought I meant that I was happy Shay and I would be friends again, but that wasn't it.

"Because it means you've forgiven me for all those months I was a fool and hurt you."

Her expression softened at my explanation. "I should have done that for Shay and for you years ago, Kane. We've been given a real second chance, and I don't want anything to tarnish that. That goes for you getting to know your brother Sebastian too. If that's what you need to do, then I'm beside you one hundred percent. Family isn't just your wife and kids. I know that."

I thought about what my father said to me in that

dream or whatever it was when I was in the hospital. Sebastian probably didn't need me in his life, but I needed to give him the chance just in case he wanted to know me as his brother.

"I don't know how I got so lucky, you know that?"

Abbi smiled. "Maybe you have a guardian angel?"

Holding her close to me, I thought about my father as my guardian angel and had to wonder. I may not have had love like my brothers had growing up, but I had it now.

And nothing was going to take that away from me.

THE END

ABOUT THE AUTHOR

K.M. Scott writes contemporary romance stories of sexy, intense, and unforgettable love. A New York Times and USA Today bestselling author, she's been in love with romance since reading her first romance novel in junior high (she was a very curious girl!). Under her Gabrielle Bisset name, she writes erotic paranormal and historical romance. She lives in Pennsylvania with a herd of animals and when she's not writing can be found reading or feeding her TV addiction.

Be sure to visit K.M.'s Facebook page at facebook.com/kmscottauthor for all the latest on her books, along with giveaways and other goodies! And to hear all the news on K.M. Scott books first, sign up for her newsletter today and be sure to visit her website at www.kmscottbooks.com.

Books by K.M. Scott:

The Corrupted Love Series
If I Dream (Corrupted Love #1)

The Heart of Stone Series
Crash Into Me (Heart of Stone #1)
Fall Into Me (Heart of Stone #2)
Give In To Me (Heart of Stone #3)
Heart of Stone Volume One Box Set
Ever After (Heart of Stone #4)
A Heart of Stone Christmas (Heart of Stone #5)
Unforgettable (Heart of Stone #6)
Unbreakable (Heart of Stone #7)
Heart of Stone Volume Two Box Set

The Club X Series
Temptation (Club X #1)
Surrender (Club X #2)
Possession (Club X #3)
Satisfaction (Club X #4)
Acceptance (Club X #5)
The Complete Club X Series Box Set

The SILK Series
SILK (Volume One)
SILK (Volume Two)
SILK (Volume Three)
SILK (Volume Four)
The SILK Box Set

K.M.'S BOOKS ARE IN AUDIOBOOK TOO!

BOOKS BY GABRIELLE BISSET:

The Sons of Navarus Series
Vampire Dreams Revamped (A Sons of Navarus Prequel)
Blood Avenged (Sons of Navarus #1)
Blood Betrayed (Sons of Navarus #2)
Longing (A Sons of Navarus Short Story)
Blood Spirit (Sons of Navarus #3)
The Deepest Cut (A Sons of Navarus Short Story)
Blood Prophecy (Sons of Navarus #4)
Blood Craving (Sons of Navarus #5)
Blood Eclipse (Sons of Navarus #6)
The Sons of Navarus Box Set #1
The Sons of Navarus Box Set #2

The Destined Ones Duology
Stolen Destiny (Destined Ones Duology #1)
Destiny Redeemed (Destined Ones Duology #2)

The Victorian Erotic Romances
Love's Master
Masquerade
The Victorian Erotic Romance Trilogy